MALEFICENCE

AN ANTHOLOGY OF QUEER DISABLED VILLAINY

An Anthology of
Queer Disabled Villainy

MALEFICENCE

Edited by
SIRIUS

Maleficence

An Anthology of
Queer Disabled Villainy

Edited by
Sirius

THE LAUGHING MAN HOUSE PUBLISHING

MALEFICENCE

"Transcendent Ruination" © 2024 by Ravven White, "The Wrong-Right Answer" © 2024 by LA Knight, "Corrupt Parrish" © 2024 by Cormack Baldwin, "Bloodlust" © 2024 by Gnosis, "Revenge of the Wild Wheeled Werebutch" © 2024 by Alex Liddell, "A Murder of Convenience" © 2024 by Tucker Struyk, "Mr. Grub" © 2024 by Sergio Palumbo, "Metu Sanguinis" © 2024 by Sarah Rossino, "A Gut Feeling" © 2024 by Kay Hanifen, "Those Who Feel No Pain" © 2024 by Sirius, "Pardon, Refuted" © 2024 by Rachel Dill, "Bored Now" © 2024 by Shannon Massey, "Inseparable" © 2024 by Toshiya Kamei

ISBN: 9798218481773

www.uncrownednovel.com

Cover Design by Sirius

Edited by Sirius

Royalty-Free images sourced by Pixabay

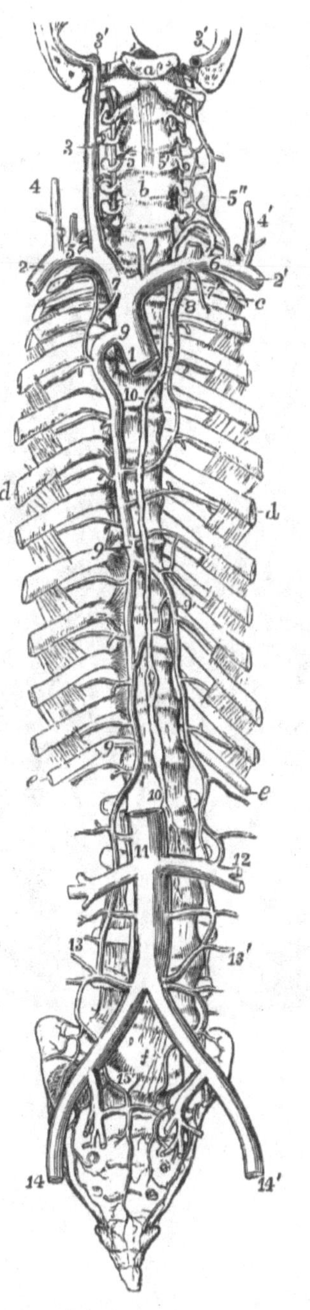

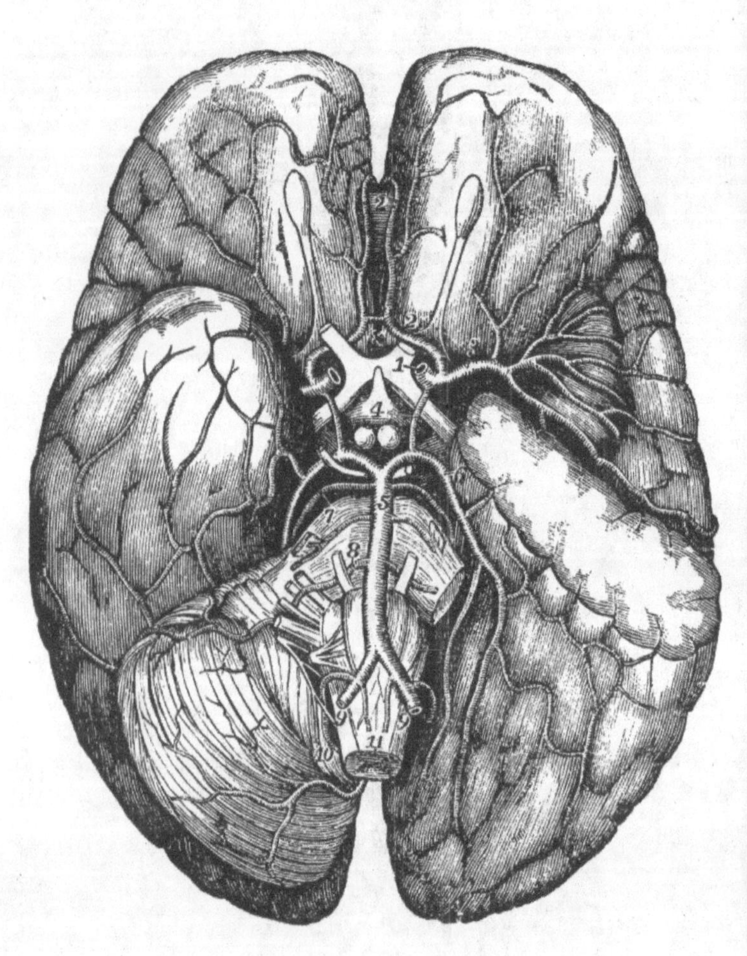

Table of Contents

Note from the Editor

This anthology was born after I spent a full week barely eating, because every bite—no matter what it was—sent me running to the toilet.

"Where are the disabled villains?" I asked my publisher after a particularly rough day. "I want to read a book where the villain has IBS."

They agreed. Chronic pain and disability are something that we share. It is something that I share with a lot of writers and artists, in fact, and yet we are always conveniently left out of large, fantastical narratives. Unless, of course, it is to make us the brunt of the joke, villainize, or fetishize us. How many villains in the stories you know are the way that they are *because* of their disability?

If you are disabled, you know what I mean. If you aren't disabled, I will ask you to name your favorite disabled character in mainstream media. Now, name three. Keep going and see how many you can name, but I think I have already well-illustrated my point as to why collections such as these are necessary.

The purpose of this anthology is to creates stories around villains are wicked *in spite* of, not *because of*, their disabilities. Do you see the difference?

Disabled characters and stories are already the main vein of my solo writing pursuits, but I wanted to bring other voices in to amplify as loudly as I could. I am only one person, after all, and I can only write for my experience and my little corner of the world. This was my first time curating an anthology all on my own, and I received submissions from across the world. That was pretty cool. I loved reading stories born from minds with different experiences, cultural backgrounds, and languages that were not my own. I did my best to do every single one of them justice, to polish them up and make them shine as brightly as possible. It was important to me that every contributor felt seen and heard.

So, this anthology is not just a celebration of disabled artists, it is also a delicious collection of queer wrongs. I could go into the politics of why queer people deserve stories that are not built around a heartwarming moral, or how so many villains are queer-coded in an attempt to, again, villainize and fetishize our queerness. But what it really boils down to is that I want to read evil gay stories, written by evil gays. Chances are that you do too, or I have to assume so, because you are here.

I hope, within these pages, you find at least one character that resonates with you.

With all my love for the disabled queers
Sincerely,
Sirius

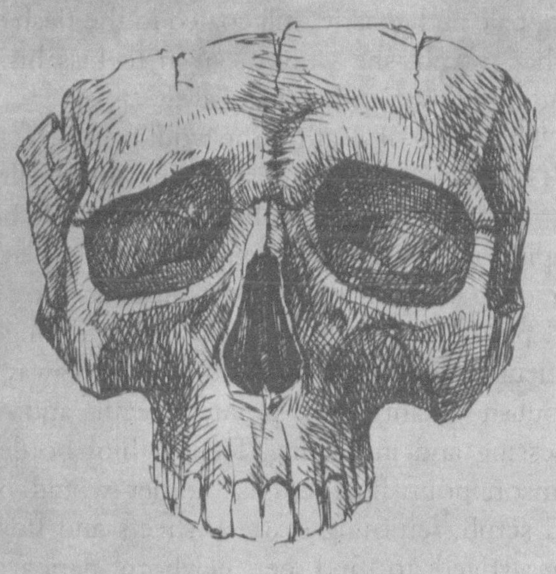

Transcendent Ruination
Ravven White

Uincent Valkane was born mean. It wasn't the fangs or bloodthirst that gave it away. It wasn't even the black pits that gazed soulless from his eye sockets. When his mother first held him, pale and ghastly, still coated in the fleshy bits of her womb, she would lean in to kiss his soft head before violently pulling away.

"He smells of death." She would gasp.

The doctors would first dismiss her, claiming that the smell was merely the bright red blood seeping into her bed sheets, the purple placenta attracting flies on the metal pan, even the sweat and piss and shit left behind from the long and difficult delivery. They would whisk away the ghoulish infant with pointed teeth and ears, assessing and inspecting, feeding him bottles of crimson nourishment. His mother would bathe and scrub, returning to fresh sheets and flowers. She arrived to find her newborn haphazardly gnawing on the placenta, ripping it into chunks, spraying blood across the fresh bed. If she had turned and run at that moment, no one would have blamed her. After all, who would want to give birth to and then raise a vicious monster? Instead, this weary woman laid down beside her creation and held him gently as he continued to devour.

The nurses would exchange worried looks as they scurried about the room. Only a handful of them at the hospital had witnessed a vampire's birth and of them, all had assisted in the baby's subsequent termination. Soon, a priest would arrive to bless the mother and absolve her of any guilt she may harbor for dispatching her horrific offspring. She would be reminded of the consequences for harboring a spawn of the devil: her family and husband would disown her, and she would lose everything on behalf of her black-eyed demon child who still smelt of death.

She would live a lonely, outcast life.

She would love her baby, regardless.

As Vincent began to grow, it became apparent that the good health and solid framework that typically accompanied a vampiric form had skipped him. He was plagued by violent reactions to blood consumption that resulted in crimson vomit and diarrhea and a perpetual growing hunger in his stomach. His mother took him to doctors and specialists who offered little help and the small sum of money she had been bequeathed out of pity soon disappeared into blood banks and black markets. She would go on to work very hard to provide her son with fresh donated blood as he responded better with nourishment from the vein rather than from a bottle or bag. She would use every resource she had, even when all that was left was her body, joining her son as a different kind of creature of the night.

Vincent would grow up around strangers that came to call—men, women, everything in between. Anyone who had the means and blood to at least partially sate him. He and his mother went through many types of blood looking for the perfect combination to ease his stomach pains and distress, but nothing ever took. As such, Vincent remained pale and thin, his body reacting to the absence of necessary nutrient absorption with underdeveloped organs and a weak spine. Vincent spent his childhood in and out of back braces, reclused to his childhood home with only his mother's 'guests' as a source to the outside world. But it wasn't even the hunger or the twisting of bones and intestine that made Vincent mean. He would spend his brief childhood relentlessly ridiculing and mocking his mother, pulling horrible pranks on her, even going so far as to wound and bruise her, giggling joyfully at her misery. His mother would endure it, for it was the only time she ever saw her demonic spawn smile, the only time she experienced his happiness. In her heart, she knew what he was, though she never named it or allowed herself to think it. She would love him, regardless.

Vincent's mother tried to hide his temperament and proclivities from the world. She would send him away during her visits, out into the fields and forests.

"You smell of death." she would tell him. "You will scare the clients away."

"You made me this way." Vincent would snarl. "Clearly your cunt is as rotten as your clientele, mother."

"I do the things I do for you, Vincent."

"You spread your whore legs for your son? Maybe you'll make me a sibling. I am deliriously hungry and a newborn babe sounds delicious."

During his banishment in the warm summer nights, he would stalk and catch local wildlife, devouring them in the woods. Something about the slurping of intestines and snapping of bones satisfied his carnal animalistic desires, even though the aftermath left him with worse gastrointestinal distress and pain than human blood. He couldn't stay away though. He craved the desperate heartbeat and terrified mewling of his victims.

Eventually his mother would stop begging for his love. She would spread her legs to whoever was willing, watch him feed on them after, and eventually succumb to red sores and a broken heart and she too would smell of death.

When she died, Vincent did not relay the message to any of her clients. When they arrived on their typical schedule, he greeted them with unusual curiosity and friendliness only to corner them in back rooms where he maliciously experimented on their bodies. The first one had been easy, never suspecting a thing as Vincent ushered him into his mother's bedroom. There, the unassuming client was greeted by the sight of her decomposing corpse as Vincent hadn't bothered to bury her. His curiosity had overtaken him and as her eyes fell from their sockets and her skin shriveled and turned green around her fingernails, he was sure he had never seen anything so beautiful. There was something about destruction that was… intoxicating. The man did not see or appreciate the beauty Vincent had displayed before him, and instead ran screaming from the room which is when Vincent captured and killed his first human victim. Many more would come after.

He started first with limbs, severing them at the joints and suckling at the exposed bones and cartilage while his victims screamed in agony and hysterical fear. Vincent would time his licks and sucks to the beat of the heart, enjoying the gush of liquids with each pulse. But they always died too quickly, their taste turning foul. Vincent dumped the bodies next to his mother's and watched in admiration as each corpse melted into the other, until all that was left was an unrecognizable heap of splintered bones and rotted flesh. He soon realized he had a fondness for bone marrow and that the thick creamy filling eased some of his stomach distress. Despite his experiments, he came to learn that nothing would never be able to compensate for his illness'. His back would always be broken, his stomach would always hurt, he would always and forever be paler and weaker than other vampires. Despite this revelation, Vincent was undeterred and unbothered. He continued collecting victims, growing a fondness for the beauty of eyes which he collected in various jars.

Eventually, Vincent ran out of clients and was forced to hunt for new prey which he felt was boring and beneath him. He'd broken enough bones, severed enough jugulars, and had become intimately knowledgeable about the areas of weakness and pain in a man. So, he left his little house in the forest and began traversing the world that had evaded him for so long. He studied it, fed on it, and determined its weakest spots. He inflicted pain whenever he had the chance, experiencing releases that were as close to the feeling he'd describe as an orgasm. Despite the hatred and disgust for his mother's profession, Vincent found himself drawn to brothels, finding beautiful specimens in dark places, whisking them away with his smooth tongue and unexplainable allure. He experimented with pain and pleasure, fucking any one he deemed beautiful, often feasting or mutilating them upon mid climax. He favored men most, especially the ones with scars adorning their chests. Vincent loved tracing his fingers along the rippled skin, followed closely by his tongue. These ones he kept alive, draining them slowly. It made him feel like a god.

He returned, briefly, to his family home, shocking the family court and forcing his father's hand. He quickly adapted to high society, despite being the bastard, monstrosity of a son. Vincent was too fast and too perceptive to be killed, and so he remained, a thorn in his father's side and a stain upon the upper class. He loved his new life, being surrounded by beautiful things and beautiful people. He adapted his style, accruing bodyguards and followers who fed off of his trickling wealth and beauty. And he was beautiful. He dressed his slender form in fine silks and stockings, tamed his golden locks in ribbons and lace, and hid the ever-lingering scent of death under rich soaps and perfumes. He acquired a glorious collection of canes and rolling chairs, ensuring his mobility with style and elegance. Eventually, he decided that his small slice of society wasn't enough, slaughtering first his father and then his siblings in secret before taking his rightful place as heir to the Valkane fortune. The Valkane's had many enemies, so their demise wasn't entirely surprising, though rumors of the vampire son seeped through, threatening Vincent's newfound kingdom. So, Vincent took his wealth and clothes, and lovers, and set his eyes on a new territory: the vampire kingdoms.

He was far too cunning and clever to waste his talent on midnight hunts, lurking in the shadows. Instead, he whispered in ears, preying on weakness, lust, and greed. He abolished monarchies without even lifting his finger and established himself as a king, poised above the frowned upon blood trades and prostitution. He settled himself in a glorious and breathtaking mansion, filled with luxurious things, and founded on torturous chambers.

And now here he stood, so many decades, centuries even, later, watching a dirty blonde, unkempt, hotheaded vampire challenge him and his existence. His throne.

And for the first time in a very long time, Vincent was charmed. Captivated.

He was dazzled by the angry, crystal blue eyes that stared him down. They were not unlike a pair he had been captivated by nearly a decade ago and he craved ownership, possession. His eyes hungrily chased a turned vampire body that had not known love or sex or pleasure, only pain and seclusion. Vincent saw something he wanted, an object that would render bliss upon defilement. He closed his eyes, weak and hard at the ruination that was awaiting him. Destructive bliss.

It would be a fun game to play, something new. Vincent couldn't quite put a reason to this sudden compulsion. He had ruined and broken plenty of vampires and humans alike and surely this one wasn't special. Maybe it was the idea of breaking that fire spirit, deflowering and dehumanizing the virginal body, reprogramming those angsty, pouting red lips to beg and plead and drool.

Or maybe it was the eyes and Vincent just wanted a matching set.

Whatever it was, Vincent had been bored for far too long. He had exhausted his experiments and tortures and had become complacent in his political maneuverings. It was as though fate had delivered this beautiful specimen right to him, to stir him from this dreary life he'd grown accustomed to. Vincent knew he must play his cards carefully. Half of the fun was the manipulation. He would not force this new toy to stay. No, he would return all on his own, under the guise of choice and freewill extended by his new master, his new and first lover, his destruction.

Vincent bid the vampire manchild goodbye when he rose to leave, savoring the look of discomfort as the crystal blue eyes met his hollow black ones. Vincent watched him leave from his balcony, secluded behind heavy cerulean velvet curtains. He would savor this, enjoy this new, beautiful treasure, climax over his broken bones, his dripping marrow, his succulent oceanic eyes. As Vincent came behind the curtains, he pondered of this new, intense obsession and decided, for the first time in his life, it must be love.

Corrupt Parrish
Cormack Baldwin

Hey Cheri
Hello, Cheri,
Dear Cheri,
I hope this letter finds
I need your help

~~I'm sorry about how I left~~
I found one of the books.

Jack tells himself that he brought the letter so he could type it out on one of the library typewriters after hours, just so the thing would be readable. Still, all he can think is pulp detective stories where they unwind the tape and out spirals a confession, clear against black ink. Exhibit A, begging help from the mistress of a gay bar downtown, its address stamped clear on the upper left. Try taking that one to court. He could argue that he's cut himself out of his old life, despite the letter, despite the fact that she's still his closest friend three months from when they last spoke.

It probably wouldn't even be the greatest of his problems. Any man who claims to have found a festering book, reeking of black flies and death and hungering to spread, would certainly be shuffled off to where he couldn't offend their senses.

He hasn't destroyed the book. He's tried. He'd found it two days ago on the shelf among academic texts on fungi, as if it had grown there. Even if he couldn't feel the twinge of something crawling in his stomach, the curse had been clear enough. The leather cover was slick with rot, already starting to puddle against the wood. Gold leaf appeared only as veins against the shadow of indents. What remained of the spine read *The Corrupt Parish.* Horseflies sought something in its binding before they, too, fell twitching to the shelf, which was now buckling under its own disintegrating wood.

He couldn't even muster indignation at its extrusion into the mundane world he'd been trying to stake out as his own. Of course the books would follow him. His first primer had warned of his death—incorrectly, as it was now 1952 and he had been slated for a car crash in 1940. Others wept blood or gibbered when opened. He'd realized early on that that didn't happen to the neighborhood kids, and he knew not to speak of it before he even had a concept of shame. The rest followed naturally. Normal people didn't look for suggestions on how to break curses in Hebrew school libraries. Normal people didn't have braces on their legs, because polio normally went away with nothing but a fever. Normal boys didn't look at the other boys like that.

Normal people don't come up with excuses about students spilling drinks to fetch a rag halfway through reshelving books, because normal people don't have to peel festering books from mold-soft covers.

But Jack Abelman did. Because if he didn't, then it would be some poor student who didn't know what not to touch melting into sludge, because that's just how this sort of thing works. Those unaware aren't protected, they're just more hapless victims. Unlike them, he knows what he's dealing with, and he has a plan.

At least, he'd *had* a plan. He'd gone home that night and tossed the book in his potbelly stove, grateful for the free tinder, even if he'd had to open every window against the smell. His apartment still reeked of sulfur when he woke up.

It was back on the shelf in the morning. Empty spaces around it suggested compatriots were being reviewed for theses and finals. Another fly shriveled atop the pages;, desiccated limbs crossed like sarcophagus depictions of long dead kings. It melted into a greenish smear, before becoming nothing more than another speck against the bubbling rot of the pages.

That night, he'd thrown the book in the fire again, and then he'd began to write.

~~This isn't me asking for pity or anything~~
~~I mean you remember the ones~~
~~I bet they don't show up at the bar anymore, thank G——~~
I'm running out of ideas of how to deal with it. I know this isn't really your ~~problem anymore~~ *wheelhouse* ~~and technically you~~

don't owe me anything, Hell, I owe you for putting me up all that time, but I need to talk to someone a spot of advice.

—————— ✦❦✦ ——————

"Margie!" Jack's fingers curl around the cotton rag he's mummified the book in for the third time. He pretends that this encounter with his boss is an unexpected delight, as opposed to the second most infuriating thing to happen today after finding the damn book. He tries to keep his smile wide. "How are you?"

"I'm doing quite alright myself." She returns a small smile, one that reveals a few straight, white teeth. "I have something to ask." She drawls out the last part, like if she keeps speaking long enough, the question itself will never have to get out.

In another life, he could demand she get to the point—tear off the bandages, spit in the wound. Instead, he says, "Anything I can help with?"

"Well, you haven't been particularly connected to the community here," she says. Her tone suggests that this is akin to handing out a death sentence. "I know you only moved recently. Have you found a church yet?"

"Have I...?" It takes him too long to process the question, much less answer it. He's never been to a church. He hasn't even been to a synagogue in a regrettable number of years. Saying the Kiddush over leftover wine was as good as he'd gotten. He'd spent most of his adult life living with Cheri, who had made clear that she found organized religion to be a scam to keep people isolated and in line, and that 'people like us' were best without it.

"If you'd like, I'm sure you'd be welcome at my church this Sunday." Margie sounds no more thrilled. Christian charity has won out again.

"Ah, well—"

Margie continues without his aborted excuses. "We need to stick together now more than ever, don't we? Now that they're letting in all of those people."

Fear and rage sink in his stomach like a swallowed stone. "Those people," Jack repeats. He wishes it was a question.

She must think it is, because she sighs. "The Jews. This place is practically crawling with them, now. I suppose the college feels bad for them."

Sometimes he wonders why he bothers. He wonders if he ought to just drop the book held so carefully behind his back. Let mold blossom out from where it lands, grow and swell in the grain of expensive hardwood flooring. Watch the rot melt the skin off of her legs before it crawls up and up and—

Even if that wouldn't kill her, he needs his job. First step on climbing the social ladder, isn't it? A new life, a clean break from the gutters. His nice, cushy job that relies on him being Christian. "No, I—I'm all sorted. I'll try to be more involved. Sorry. Still adjusting." He tells himself that the bile in his throat is a side effect of the thing dripping in his hands. He tells himself the burning of his palms is in his mind.

The relief is palpable, and he hates her for it. "Glad to hear."

He lies well wishes though his teeth as she returns to wherever it is she came. As soon as she's gone, he stashes the book in his bag and shoves the whole thing on the bottom of his cart. He'll figure it out later. If only everything could just happen later.

~~How many times can I burn this~~ I've tried ~~burning~~ the usual method two times now and drowning a third time. ~~The rot bubbled to the surface, turning the whole thing thick and musky, like pond scum. For a beautiful moment, I thought the thing had finally dissolved.~~

I ~~can't go home without people noticing~~ don't have ~~the wherewithal~~ time to visit, I'm sorry. I'm at a loss for how to fix this.

~~I miss you~~

~~I love you~~
I look forward to your reply,
Jack

⤛⬥⬥⬥⬥⬥⬥⤜

The book is waiting for him again as he returns from posting the letter. He's become resigned to its presence. For a moment, he considers just leaving it. There won't be any consequences, not on his head. There's nothing that's keeping him from letting it spread beyond the mucus drooling off the side of the shelf. He could walk away and deny he ever saw it when the shelf collapses and dissolves into rot, along with half the floor.

He shakes his head and grabs a new rag from his bag. He's not sure what mitzvah not killing one's charges through neglect of an evil object that wishes them to return to the supple earth falls under, but he can't be wrong 613 times in a row. Tikkun olam, something like that.

He's thrown out of his thoughts by a bony shoulder bumping into his. He can't suppress a yelp as the book is jostled out of his hand. Out of instinct, he grabs for it with the hand that had been on the cart. His fingers grip the covered spine just in time, but without the support, his bad leg buckles despite the brace, and his head cracks against the floor. The world becomes a sunburst of light and pain.

"Oh, I am *so* sorry!" The voice is too young to be faculty, and sure enough, when his vision clears, a girl who looks barely out of high school is covering her mouth. "I'm so, so sorry. Let me help you up—" she reaches down, hand extended.

For an addled moment, he pulls away, convinced she's about to grab the book and dissolve into rot. Reason seeps in slowly, and he forces something approximating a laugh. "Ah, sorry, just a moment." He'd like the help up, but doing so would require both dropping the book and admitting to her that he can't do it on his own.

"Are you sure?" she asks, her voice still an octave above what sounds natural. Her eyes widen as he sits up, sliding the book onto the bottom shelf of his cart to free his hands. "Oh my goodness, is your foot alright?"

It takes him a second longer to realize that she's staring at the bottom of his brace, revealed by the riding up of his slacks. The metal fastener connecting the leather ankle strap to his shoe, usually ignorable under his pantlegs, shines against the flickering library lights. Suddenly, the lifted shoe, its compatriot long ago worn to holes, stands out against the poorly-matched one on his good leg. "It's fine. I—" he debates whether secrecy or honesty will get him further as he grabs the nearest shelf and prays his weight won't break the bracket, "I had polio as a child. I'm fine, really."

Her hand goes from her mouth to her heart. "You're a polio? That's awful, I'm so sorry. There was a girl in my sixth form who was one, too, and she nearly died. I didn't realize people like you had jobs, you know? That's so impressive." Her voice is low, tentative.

The shelf creaks, but he gets far enough up to grab the cart again and regain his balance. He's not sure how to respond, nor does he want to. What's the proper response to a stranger nearly dying? He wonders what she thinks happens 'people like him' when they get out of the ward. Sequestered in institutions further from her pretty little schools? Evaporate into thin air? He wonders what would happen if he told her his job before was at a gay bar, whether he'd still be impressive. At the same time, he can't even find fault in her for it. It's probably what runs through the head of every patron that sees him walk.

"It can be dangerous," he intones.

Neither of them is pleased with the answer. Her eyes are still on the fastener, now the only visible part of his brace. At least she isn't looking at the book, which is now leaking brackish decomposition through the worn cotton. The metal shelving of the cart blossoms into rust.

He clears his throat as politely as he can, hoping to end the conversation before the cart corrodes through and he has much more to explain.

"Well, sorry again. I'll see you later?" she asks, still speaking to his shoe.

"As long as you keep up your studies," he confirms.

She scurries away, and he wonders how much he needs to pad the book before it stops seeping through.

Jack—

Jesus, academia has done a number on you. Unless it's the curse that's saying 'spot of advice' like this is some upper crust business luncheon? Haha, it's okay, you're allowed to be a stick in the mud. I'm sure your new university friends love it. Maybe they're why you haven't even sent a postcard in months, hmm?

Anyways, I don't really remember most of the ways you dealt with the books. You set a couple of my trash cans on fire, but you said you already tried that. Drowning was also good, glad that wasn't in my tub this time. I'm guessing it's not one of the ones you can wrap up and ignore. After that, have you tried cutting it up and scattering the bits? Maybe instead of water, put it in vinegar or something. I think you buried one of the ones that showed up when you lived with me.

Really, though. I'm happy to help, but you do know you can still come home, right?

Good luck,
Cheri

ack cringes as he pours a quarter of paycheck's worth of vinegar down the sink.

He's not sure what he expected. He tried cutting it, but it only squelched under his knife before healing back together like a wound knitting closed. He'd scooped out the softest pieces, bit by bit, grinning as pits formed under his pick. His weekend had dissolved into a sleepless frenzy, scratching and scraping, cleaning until his hands were raw from the soap and water.

He is broken. The book is the same, always crumbling.

Just breathing the air of his flat stings as he realizes that he has five minutes before he'll be late for work. *The Corrupt Parish* sits, a gelatinous mass, in a scrounged cake tin. It sighs globs of slime among bubbling acid. Rust inches across the metal beneath it. There's no way he can bring it, and no way he can leave it behind. He considers going down to the front desk and borrowing the phone to call in. His voice will be raw enough from the vinegar fumes to feign illness. It's the evening shift, with the holidays fast approaching. It's not like a college missing their assistant librarian will herald in the apocalypse.

Then again, calling in right before he's set to arrive will set off the whispers he can feel right behind his back. Wasn't it cruel to hire him, anyways? A man in his condition. He never fit in anyways. Have you noticed that? Haven't you seen? Or maybe it'll ripple further, until all of 'those people' are condemned for their laziness. Until he collapses and the delicate structure tumbles.

The rust creeps up the walls of his sink, turning to fingers of mold as it hits the counter. The burn of vinegar turns to sickly sweetness, changes again to a rich bitter that tickles the back of his throat and makes him gag. He wants to fall to his knees. He wants to vomit until this horrible thing has been purged from every cell.

He does not. Black lines of thread-like fungi spill from racing cracks in the concrete. The bricks of the kitchen shed blond dust before chunks fall with a quiet *plop plop plop* into the swamp spilling from the sink. The ceiling above him groans.

The air itself feels septic, on the verge of breaking. His eyes burn from the cleanliness and the rot. He wants to fix this. He wants to go home. He wants to die.

He's not sure what he wants as he walks away.
He just knows that he has to go to work.

Inseparable
Toshiya Kamei

A horrible nausea wakes me, replacing a vivid dream where I was intimate with Rosa. All is dark except for the red glow of the clock radio by the bed. It's not quite 5 a.m. The stifling air of a San Antonio summer wraps around my skin. I nudge my sister, who lies asleep next to me.

"Wake up, Daisy." I reach for the bedside lamp and switch it on.

"Gosh, Violet." She stirs and groans, her eyes still closed. "What's wrong now?"

"I'm sick." Tears sting my eyes, taking me by surprise. I brush away a few strands of dark curly hair sticking to her forehead. "I'm going to throw up."

I hate doing this, but I have no choice. My sister and I are inseparable, literally joined at the hip like our namesakes, the Hilton sisters. Like San Antonio's original conjoined twins, we have to go everywhere together.

Trying to throw off the dregs of slumber, Daisy blinks a few times. Synchronized, we crawl out of bed and stagger toward the bathroom.

I lift the toilet seat right before I puke up my guts. The scent of violets penetrates my nostrils. I gag as bile rises in my throat again, and blue petals cloud the bowl.

"I hate this," I say. Saliva drooling from my mouth, I wipe the tears that follow the retching. "It's horrible."

Daisy doesn't speak as we stand, but I can feel concern radiating off of her. We half-shuffle, half-stumble to the sink, and I lean over the basin to splash my face with cold water.

"Don't tell me you have hanahaki disease again," Daisy says as I look in the mirror. "Who's your crush this time?"

My reflection makes me cringe. There are bags under my eyes, and my cheeks are hollowed. I try to run my fingers through my bleached blonde hair, but it's too tangled and matted. I can't stop staring, temporarily blocking my sister out of my mind.

"Who is it?" Daisy asks again. Slightly shorter and plumper, she's the demurer one. Our gazes lock in the mirror before I avert my eyes and sigh.

"I don't want to talk about it." Dread chokes me as I recall what happened to my last crush, Leticia. How can I forget? She sat behind us in calculus in our senior year at Alamo Heights High. Needless to say, things didn't go well between us. I grimace at the memory of Leticia's face twisting when I asked her out.

"Why not, Violet? We share everything."

I say nothing.

We drop our pajama bottoms and sit on the toilet. We share a bladder, which is a source of annoyance, but the steady flow of pee calms my nerves.

"Alright," I say, resigned, and flush the toilet before we leave the bathroom. "It's Rosa. I'm having bubbly wondrous dreams about her."

"Bubbly wondrous?" Daisy asks. "Oh, Sis, you sound like a Neutral Milk Hotel song." Mom is the one who is into Jeff Mangum's band. She's so fanatical that she once made a pilgrimage to Ruston, the small Louisiana town where Mangum was born.

Rosa is a nursing student from Mexico. Mom hired her as our live-in caregiver when we moved into our own apartment. I told Mom we could look after ourselves, but she insisted.

"Gee, Violet," Daisy says as we crawl back into bed. "I don't think she's queer."

I shake my head, frowning.

"Not even remotely." Daisy stabs me with her verbal knife. "She never flirts back," she adds, as if to twist her blade before withdrawing.

"I thought she was playing hard to get," I say with feigned cheer.

"You're hopeless, Violet."

"I am?"

Daisy sighs before turning off the lights.

"Do you think she's still seeing that guy?" I lower my voice, recalling the bruises Rosa used to hide under long sleeves.

"I don't know."

"We should do something about him." We once followed Rosa to her boyfriend's apartment on Vance Jackson Road. While we spied from our parked car, Rosa ran out of the front door in tears.

We heard him yell after her and slam the door. She wiped her face, made a tearful apology, and went back in before we could intervene. I regret that we didn't do anything then.

"Go back to sleep, Violet."

"I don't know if I can."

Daisy sighs again. Silence falls, broken only by the soft breathing of my sister drifting off.

Even with my eyes shut, disquieting thoughts keep circulating through my mind.

Besides the bladder, we also share a sacrum, rectum, and reproductive organs. That hurts our dating prospects. Even so, we both remain optimistic about finding love. We take comfort in the fact that the Bunker brothers, the original Siamese twins, married two sisters and fathered over twenty children.

Despite being twins, we're so different from each other. We used to give Mom a hard time by refusing to dress identically.

Speaking of sharing, I wasn't the only one carrying a torch for Leticia. Daisy also had the hots for Miss Popularity, even though she refused to admit it. Lucky for her, my sister isn't as susceptible to hanahaki disease as I am, and she didn't become sick like I did. When I first coughed up petals, my health spiraled out of control. I could hardly breathe as the violets grew in my heart and lungs, and pollen found its way throughout my circulatory system. Daisy had no choice but to help me. We cornered Leticia in the girls' bathroom after school, but romance was a no-go.

When I told Mom about my hanahaki disease, she said I had to think about my sister as well. If I died before Daisy, she'd have to undergo surgical separation. Mom opined that it'd be the height of irresponsibility for me to expose my sister to such a danger. Alas, Leticia had to die. A popular cheerleader, she was elected homecoming queen posthumously our senior year.

Unable to fall back asleep, I grab my phone and check my email. My inbox shows one new message. It's Mom, informing me she's sent us a postcard by Deutsche Post. She must be the only one sending real paper cards these days. She's old-fashioned like that.

Mom had been excited to learn she was pregnant. As soon as she'd found out she was expecting twins, she settled on Daisy and Violet. Both are common flowers, but very pretty.

Mom didn't think of the connection at that time, but Daisy and Violet Hilton, British-born conjoined twins who had played vaudeville in the 1920s, lived in San Antonio after coming to America.

However, Mom's fourteen-week scan had revealed she was carrying conjoined twins. The doctors had told her the pregnancy was high-risk and had recommended she have an abortion.

Around seven o'clock, my phone vibrates, signaling another email. It's Mom again. In a frank and drunk tone, she says she and her wife arrived in Heidelberg by night train. While traveling in Germany, they visited an old brick mansion that resembled the Hilton sisters' old residence in San Antonio.

The sisters had entered show business before turning three, and they eventually settled in San Antonio and performed at theaters downtown. They also appeared in Tod Browning's 1932 horror film *Freaks*. Unlike our namesakes, we're not artistically inclined. We're rather ordinary college students, both majoring in education at UTSA.

Doctors have explained to us that we could have been separated in surgery, but Mom had decided against it because there had been a good chance only one of us would have survived. She had been unable to bear the thought of losing one of us.

A half hour later, Rosa enters the bedroom after a few knocks on the door.

"Buenos días," Rosa says with a smile.

"Buenos días," Daisy replies, stretching her arms above her head.

"¿Cómo amanecimos?" Rosa asks. As she walks to the window, I follow her with my eyes, admiring her dusky complexion. Dressed in navy blue scrubs, she wears her jet-black hair in a tight bun that's accentuated by her nurse's cap. She slides the curtains open, and a bright light bathes the room.

"Muy bien," I lie. Even so, seeing Rosa's smile alleviates my symptoms, albeit temporarily.

As usual, Rosa takes our vital signs and asks about our bowel movements before leaving for her nursing school.

We take a shower and get dressed. I put on a floral summer dress, pale blue with yellow flowers, and Daisy wears a white crop top and dark denim shorts.

After a quick bowl of cereal, we leave for the John Peace Library where we work as library assistants.

The campus is empty except for those taking summer courses. Once inside the building, we heave a sigh of relief. It's a great place to take shelter from the summer heat.

When we step into the medical section, Daisy pulls a dusty title off a shelf. The gold leaf letters on the spine read 'Physicians' Guide to Rare Disorders.'

"This is far from being my cup of tea," I say. "Good thing I have a brainy sister."

Daisy rolls her eyes, exasperated. We return to the entrance area and sit behind the circulation desk. It's silent except for the pages rustling as Daisy flips through the book.

"Anything interesting?" I ask.

"Yeah," she says. "There's a case study of an inhaled pea. A retired teacher had a pea plant growing in his lung. He'd been short of breath for months, coughing a lot and feeling listless. Sound familiar?"

A hacking cough threatens to rise in my throat every few minutes, and I imagine the violets blooming inside my lungs. I hold my handkerchief to my mouth, trying to stifle the cough.

"Are you alright?" Daisy asks, looking up from her book.

I unfold the cloth and show her a single petal inside.

"You're not getting better, are you?" She says, tilting her head. "The good news is that hanahaki disease isn't infectious."

"That's good to know." It's my turn to roll my eyes.

"Let's get serious," she says. "We have to do something about Rosa."

"Wait, I have an idea," I say in haste. "If we can get the boyfriend is out of the picture…"

"Violet, sweetheart." Daisy cuts in. "Do you really expect Rosa to fall in love with you?"

"Do you have a better idea?" I ask, feeling desperate.

She says nothing, but I know what she's thinking. I remember the horror that flashed across Leticia's eyes before she died. No. I can't go that route again. I can't bear losing Rosa, let alone hurting her. I shudder at the thought. I don't deserve such a cruel fate. Don't I deserve happiness like everyone else?

"No, Daisy," I say, stifling the urge to scream. "I don't want to hurt Rosa. She's been so good to us."

"Yes, I know, but we don't have a lot of choices."

I silently concede she's right.

It was Daisy's idea to work in the library. While she prefers burying her nose in a book, I enjoy chatting with patrons. If this job has an unexpected benefit, it's that we look less conspicuous behind the circulation desk.

In the evening, we pick up Rosa at San Antonio College and head downtown. The cough is gone. My proximity to Rose seems to temporarily mitigate my hanahaki disease.

Daisy and I drive in tandem: I'm in charge of the gas and the brakes, and I let my sister steer most of the time. Funny how things work out. A fun fact: we each had to take the test when we got our licenses.

We finally find a parking spot on the street. We leave our cane in the trunk as we want to practice walking without it.

Accompanied by Rosa, we stroll along the Paseo del Rio, winding through the heart of downtown. The pathway is lined with gift shops, cafés, and restaurants on the banks of the San Antonio River. The heat of summer hasn't abated in the least, even after the sunset.

Growing up, Daisy and I had to learn to crawl together and then walk together. After years of practice, we can walk without communicating verbally. Even so, we're far from being graceful.

Walking requires a lot of effort, even now. The easiest analogy that comes to mind is a three-legged race. In short, we have to coordinate our movements.

We can't help attracting stares from strangers, but Rosa's presence has the effect of dissimulating our weirdness. I'm grateful to Rosa for that. We enter Lone Star Cafe and sit at a table by the window. When a waitress comes over, we order three glasses of iced coffee and three pieces of pecan pie. I cast my gaze outside as out-of-town visitors meander among cypress trees and stone walls.

"Tengo que decirte algo, Rosa," I say. Mom wants us to brush up on our Spanish with Rosa. We used to speak good Spanish, but we've fallen out of practice since Abuela passed away a decade ago.

The waitress returns with our order. I sip my drink and try to quench my thirst. I wonder if Daisy is as thirsty as I am.

Daisy opens her book and begins reading. It's *In the Dream House*, Carmen Maria Machado's 2019 memoir about domestic abuse.

"Dime," Rosa says, urging me to go on. Her brown eyes shine with curiosity.

I sit up, staring at her. One of Taylor Swift's love songs comes on. It's about a girl who's in love with her best friend. I know it's crazy, but I take it as a sign. I want to reach out and caress Rosa's face.

"Estoy enamorada de ti," I blurt my confession, feeling my cheeks flush.

"Ay, pobrecita." Pity tinges her voice, and I wince. "Tú lo que estás es confundida."

"Pero no estoy confundida," I say. "Tú eres mi cura." I know it's a corny thing to say, but Rosa is literally my cure.

Rosa remains silent, giving me a bewildered look. It turns out she's the one who's confused, not me.

"¿Cómo está tu novio?" I ask, changing the subject. I don't know her boyfriend's name. Even if I did, I'd never mention it.

"Muy bien."

I then notice a bruise on her wrist, barely visible. My heart sinks as I recall a time when Rosa sported a two-day-old black eye, insisting she had fallen.

"¿Qué te pasó?" I ask, frowning.

"Nada," Rosa says, pulling away. "No te preocupues."

Daisy and I exchange worried glances. We go to the restroom to empty our caffeine-riddled bladder.

"It's high time we pay the boyfriend a visit," I say as I close the door behind us.

That night, we drive in silence to Rosa's boyfriend's apartment. No longer able to endure the silence, I turn on the car radio. Another Taylor Swift song plays, this one with a reference to star-crossed lovers. I know our stars will align once the boyfriend is out of the way. I'll be with Rosa soon, comforting her in my arms.

Reaching our destination, we get out of the car, open the trunk, and take out the cane. We walk to the door and knock a few times. A goateed man our age answers. He wears a Spurs jersey and shorts.

"What do you want?" he asks, frowning. His breath smells of tobacco.

"Is Rosa here?" Daisy asks.

"No." He shakes his head. "What are you anyway?" He sneers. "Did you run away from the circus or something?"

When we take a step forward, he tenses.

"She didn't tell you about us?" I ask. Anger festers like a blister, threatening to burst.

"No," he says curtly and glances at us with contempt.

Before he can close the door, we bash his head in with the cane. He falls to one knee with a groan, and blood trickles down his forehead. Adrenaline rushes into our extremities. Goosebumps ripple from our legs to our heads, and our hearts race. Another blow topples him to the ground. We shove him inside and shut the door behind us.

When he stirs, we club him again and again until he stops moving. A thrilling sensation runs through our bodies. Our heartbeats pump louder and louder. With each beat, our vision flickers.

We drag his limp body to the bathroom and lift him into the tub. The semi-clear shower curtain has a slight moldy odor. Sitting on the edge of the tub, we check his pulse. Nothing. We wait for a few minutes. Nothing. Dainty and dirty emotions surge through me before they fade away.

I suddenly want to pee. Our bladder is so enlarged I can feel it pressing against our bellybutton. We draw the curtain around the tub, sit on the toilet, and pee.

My phone beeps with an incoming call, startling me. It's Mom. I put her on speaker so Daisy can hear.

"How are you girls?" Mom says, euphoric. Some of the tension eases at the timbre of her voice.

"Glorious and fine," Daisy says, echoing Jeff Mangum's lyrics.

"The Black Forest is a precious place to visit," Mom says.

"Send us photos, Mom," I say.

I imagine the petals melting away inside me like a curse being broken. Relieved, we leave the corpse in the tub and drive home.

The Wrong-Right Answer
L.A. Knight

White wine mixed with blood like new-minted coins spreads across my tongue. Like quicksilver promises, like betrayal.

After twenty years, I don't know what to do with myself if I can't taste that blood.

It doesn't have to be *my* blood. Shadowlord Rook taught me that.

⁓⊹⊱❈⊰⊹⁓

"Do you want to go home?" My words echo off the black marble of my great hall. *Home, home, home.* A quicksilver-sweet lie like the blood of fallen heroes on my lips.

"Wh-what?" The Chosen One has such a squeaky little voice. And a stutter like my own. Coming out now because I've gone off her expected script? Or fear? Or both?

"Do you want to go home?"

A question with claws and fangs. I ask it of every Chosen One who dares to come knocking. This little hero doesn't know which answer will bring my teeth crunching down on her skinny stem of a throat.

This would-be savior is barely a child.

Why did the treacherous gods send a child to kill a queen? Surely even they can't be so cruel.

Surely, they know her age won't stay my vengeance.

There is so much blood on the floor. Deep, black pools of it catching the light of moonstone lamps. The air stinks of rust and viscera.

I can practically feel it caking thick under my fingernails; it makes me itch to tear my skin off.

"Well?"

I want this interrogation over so I can either enchant her or initiate her. So my minions can take the gasping, bleeding not-yet-dead soldiers to my laboratory and throw the no-those-are-actually-dead ones into our chasm.

"Answer the question, little hero. Do—you—want—to—go—home?"

Nobody asked me that question before sending me to fight Shadowlord Rook. Maybe the gods knew if they had, I'd have given the wrong answer.

She glares, eyes burning icy as the darkest pits in this world's thirteenth Hell. Such spit and fury. If she gives me the right-wrong answer, her soul will fuel my anchor-spell for a long, long time.

This newest hero is a sprawly thing, all legs and elbows and those glacial sapphire eyes glowing with magic behind glasses as thick as my own. Hair chopped in a glossy brown bowl-cut. Skinny as a stick. Did they feed her at that temple? If she's underfed, she may not last as long in the lab. Damn.

"You're not gonna just let me go back to the temple. I'm not fall—"

Oh, for fuck's sake.

"Earth, you obnoxious b-brat." And there's *my* stutter because I'm deviating from *my* script. "Do you want, want to g-go home *to Earth?*"

Hate twists her face, and an odd hurt. She clutches her pitiful sword.

"Stop m-m-making f-fun of me!"

For a second, I have no idea what in the Thirteen Hells she's talking about. Then I realize— my stutter only comes out when I don't use my practiced scripts. The bratling hasn't heard it before.

"Do I l-look like someone who'd m-make fun of a stutter?"

Maybe it's an unfair question. Maybe she doesn't realize I'm in my beautiful fangstone Chair not because I'm bored with this, but because I need it to get around my castle. Wouldn't do for the infamous Carrion Swan to faint every time she strolls down a hallway. Last thing I need is to smash my skull open on my lovely floor.

My Chair rumbles, a rough-velvet purr like a lion. It wants to feed on this girl's blood as much as my anchor-spell wants to feed on her soul.

I could've requisitioned a regular wheelchair when the anemia started interfering with my day-to-day activities. I wanted one forged of sentient fangstone. Something that *fights* for me, not just helps me get around. Something that matches the figure I cut in my white silk and leather.

A few squamous, burgundy tentacles stretch out from the base of the Chair toward the spreading pool of hero-blood.

The Chosen One hefts her sword. "St-stay back!"

My jaw aches. I've got to stop grinding my teeth during these confrontations.

"How old are y-you?"

She blinks.

"Eighteen?"

Spoken like a question. Like a lie. I guess fifteen, *maybe* sixteen.

Whatever.

"Do you know why you're here?" Easier to swallow the stutter if I stick with the script I've practiced with Rook for the last decade.

"T-to defeat you, Carrion Swan! To f-free Portalis from you! To avenge every White Raven before me that you've murdered! Then drag you in chains before the gods to meet your punishment!" Her voice gets stronger with every word, the stutter fading. Fear then, not impediment.

To avenge every White Raven. So, the gods are still peddling that sanctimonious bullshit to every would-be miracle child they snatch from Earth. Does this little hero think I've killed every White Raven, every Chosen One called before her?

Does she know who I really am?

"You're here," I say coldly, "because the gods want a villain, and they want a hero who'll be a good little dog and do everything they command. I'm the villain," I cross a leg over one knee and smirk, a practiced move straight out of *The Evil Overlord Manual* that Rook brought from Earth all those years ago. "*You're* the dog. Bark, heel, fetch. And once you're done, do you know what the gods will do with their dog?"

You're just the errand dog of the gods, White Raven. They're using you. They'll use you up.

Old words. Old wounds. Scars that still split and bleed whenever I'm forced to have this thrice-damned conversation.

"I'll be their high priestess," the Chosen One shoots back. "I'll—"

"They'll send you back."

She stares at me.

"They'll dump you back in your normal, boring, mundane life and forget all about you. Every connection you've made here, every memory, every dream—gone. Even your *body* will no longer be yours. It will be the old, discarded thing you had when you first arrived, before you grew into your realness."

Then comes the typical tantrum, about how I'm a liar, and the gods have *Chosen* her, and she'll save the world from my tyranny, and blah blah blah.

The right-wrong answer. The one I hoped she wouldn't give.

Oh, well.

Another reason I have this conversation sitting down? Five times out of ten, I have to hurt people. I have a hard enough time being on my feet when I'm *not* doing magic to turn people's blood to acid or shatter their magic shields into fragments; I'm sure as Hell not going to start throwing magic at someone when I might faint at any moment.

It takes two quick shots of brilliant blue light from a casually flicked finger to send the little hero sprawling into a pool of half-congealed blood. Her head thuds against the floor. A wound in her side starts to soak scarlet into her tunic.

"Shall I transport her for you, my lady?"

I lean back with a sigh and a tired smile. Not the way I wanted this confrontation to end, but at least I've got more fuel for my anchor-spell.

"Yes. Thank you, dear heart," I say to Kestrel. My Kestrel, so beautiful, like a shard of midnight forged into the perfect woman. She towers over me by a foot, all the ample curves of a fertility goddess and the lethal skills of a trained assassin. The first Chosen One to hunt me down after I joined with Shadowlord Rook.

Unlike the girl on the floor, Kestrel had given me the wrong-right answer to my question.

Do you want to go home?

Rook had asked me that, two decades ago. My answer had been the same as Kestrel's: *Portalis* is *my home.*

My fangstone Chair slurps up the blood trail spilling from the little hero as Kestrel drags the sobbing child to my lab, throws her on a pallet in the center of a magical nexus, and hooks her into the anchor-spell. Young as she is, I might get a few years out of her soul before it snuffs out.

"Should've said…n-no," I murmur to the weeping girl. Tendrils of white light dance over her skin, sipping away her life.

"Whaaa…" She's already drifting into unconsciousness.

"When…asked if…wanted to g-go home, back to Earth." I sigh as she faints. "Should've said no."

I wonder what her name was.

It doesn't really matter, I suppose.

#

"Do you want to go home?"

Shadowlord Rook asked me the question for the third time as I tied another series of intricate knots around his wrists and ankles. Blood trickled from cuts and slashes on his arms and face. I didn't care; he deserved them all. He deserved worse.

"Portalis is home." If he wasn't going to stop asking, I had to give him an answer to shut him up.

"They're going to send you back to Earth."

My head snapped up.

"Shut your mouth! You can't trick me! The gods warned me you were a deceiver."

"They should know." His golden-brown face twisted into a grimace. He licked away a drip of blood at the corner of his mouth. "They forged us both into what we are."

I was so certain in that moment that he was lying.

I wasn't a child, but I was a fool.

The next Chosen One finds me in my bedroom after my bath. Rude of him.

"I'm here to bring an end to your tyranny, Carrion Swan!"

And foolish, giving me a warning. I raise both hands. Jay, the youth carefully running a wide-toothed pick through my tight, black curls, sets the pick down and backs up against the far wall; Crane, the girl strumming a harp in the corner, stills her strings at my gesture and scurries to stand next to Jay.

I roll words and sarcasm around in my mouth for a few moments, then ask slowly, "Didn't they teach you how to knock at that temple?"

"Stand up! Face me!"

I set my hands on the gently vibrating arms of my fangstone Chair, and it turns toward this bratling boy. He's even younger than the last one. Maybe fourteen? His voice hasn't broken yet. What are the gods thinking, sending striplings after me?

"Stand up," I echo. "Is that…a joke?"

I *can* stand, but it's an ordeal of tingling extremities, dizziness, roaring in my ears, increasingly severe stutter, brain fog, all the anemic annoyances. I certainly don't do it for every upstart fool who waltzes into my castle.

"Fight me! Murderer!" He advances with sword bared. Steel polished to gleam like silver in the light of moonstone lamps. He's stork-tall, milk-pale knobby wrists and pink ears that stick out from his shaved head. Twiggy arms shake with the effort of holding the gleaming sword.

Script time.

"Do you want to go home?"

He stumbles. The sword dips. "What?"

"Do you want to go home?"

How many times am I going to have to repeat myself to these obnoxious *children* swinging their sharp, stabby objects at me?

I am so tired.

"What do you mean? *Portalis* is my home."

I blink. For the first time in a long while, the wrong-right answer instead of the right-wrong one. Maybe this stripling has a chance.

"You don't want to return to Earth?"

Crane and Jay flinch at the edge of my vision, grip each other's hands. Animal recognition of the sting in the tail of this scorpion-question. I asked them the same thing once.

"No!" A single word soaked in panic. "And you can't send me back! The gods will protect me from your magic!"

From behind him, my beloved Kestrel asks, "You sure about that, bratling?"

The hero whips toward her; she's wise enough to stand back from him. No accidental, tragic swipe of his little sword will end *my* consort.

"Stand back," the boy-hero snarls. "This is between me and the Swan."

"The gods won't protect you," Kestrel says flatly. "They're using you. They want you to capture my lady and drag her back to their accursed temple of games and lies. Once you—"

"Shut up!"

The little bastard actually swings his hatpin of a sword at my beloved.

Kestrel dodges the quick arc of silvery light easily. She's done this almost as many times as I have.

She's the only Chosen One to ever beat me in combat.

"Not smart, little brat," my Kestrel says. Her smile is like white bone against polished midnight, an ivory knife in the dark.

"They warned me," his voice cracks on *warned*, and I have to swallow the fury churning in my belly, aimed at gods that keep sending nuisances to my fortress. "They told me you'd try to turn me against them! You can't trick me!"

Well. A new-old move on the chessboard. They haven't tried this since I ran away with Rook.

"They…warned you?"

It's been a good several days. No fainting spells, not even any dizziness or tightness in my chest. I brace my hands on the vibrating arms of my Chair and push slowly to my feet.

Pride, maybe. Curiosity, certainly. Maybe I just…forget myself for a few moments, presented with this new-old thing that makes me want to shield this child behind a wall of glass hellthorn because they've already warped his mind in a familiar way; makes me want to sink my talons into this hero's wrists and pry the answers out of him while crimson drips on the marble floor because he's the enemy now and he's probably not going to listen.

It's not boredom, whatever else it might be. That in itself is a new step in the old dance.

"What…did they say?"

His sword points at me now. Kestrel watches from behind; when she glances to me, I shake my head. Not yet.

"That you'll try to make me think the gods will betray me—"

"They will," I say flatly, "but okay."

"Liar!"

There's a waver there. Not just his voice breaking. Uncertainty. I pounce on it, catch it between my teeth as I risk a step away from my Chair.

"The gods don't reward loyalty. You don't want to go back to Earth," I say. Old words, worn into my tongue and my bones. "I can make sure you don't. We won't let them send you back. Forget the gods. Stay with us."

He wavers again. His uncertainty, his longing, they pulse in my mouth like a heart caught in my jaws.

Then I bite down, off-script. I'm starting to get dizzy; I need to hurry this up.

"Join me."

A mistake.

Amateur. Shadowlord Rook's voice, though he's nowhere in sight. Memory or thought-sending? No time to figure it out because the stripling's eyes turn to flint. He swings his silvery sword gleaming with moonstone glow…and another glow.

He's feet away. I have just enough time to think, *Oh. Magic sword. Fuck.*

Then the spell slams into my chest. Hot copper spills thick into my throat as my feet lift from the floor. I hear Kestrel's agonized cry. My servants shout something.

I smash into my floor in a pile of light brown limbs and white pajamas. Pain shockwaves through my back. My head smacks the thick, dark wyrdwolf rug in front of my fireplace; the only thing that stops my brains from splashing across the fur.

Can't breathe. Sparkles flash across my vision. A scream claws at my throat. My spell. My *spell*. It's *failing?* Light and shadow writhe before my eyes. Earth roars in my ears like a fiend, trying to drag me back to it.

A single sob crawls out of me.

"Raven!"

Kestrel is on her knees next to me. A thousand braids fall in a dark curtain around my tingling face.

Did the hero's magic send *her* back to Earth too? Am I about to lose her? We came through the Portalis Door at different times, I don't know how to find her on Earth! I should've planned for this, but I…and the others, there won't be anyone to protect them, I should have—

The rainbow sparks fade as I take a breath. The wyrdwolf fur is soft under my head. The floor is cold and hard.

My *elbows* hurt?

And my butt. Very much my butt.

Right. The stripling threw me with a spell. I'm not being pulled back to my birth World. I'm just oxygen-deprived.

I suck in a breath. Another. The roaring of my blood in my ears fades, replaced by…a very ominous squelching noise, punctuated with wet cracking sounds.

"Thirteen Hells," I mumble as Kestrel helps me sit up. Pain twinges in my hips and butt. My head *throbs* like a rotten tooth. "M'okay. I'm…oh. P-Please don't, don't cry, Kes." Shit.

"You're so damn *stupid*," she sobs, squeezing me hard enough my back pops. I deserve it for frightening her. Still…

"That's n-n-not a nice way to, to talk to y-your liege, Kestrel."

"Shut up."

I'd hug her back, but my shoulders don't want to work. I probably only flew about five or so feet, since I didn't crash into a wall, but I'm going to be a patchwork quilt of bruises in the morning, and stiff as a corpse.

The squelching and cracking get louder.

Right. Have to deal with that.

A quick look past Kestrel shows what I expect: Jay has the Chosen One pinned; Crane stabs him over and over with the dirk all my people carry. Silent tears stream down her copper-brown cheeks. Blood spatters her blue sleeves.

Well. Not going to be able to use *him* for my spell.

I manage to make myself heard over the sound of metal slicing through guts and the cracking of bones.

"Crane!"

Her head jerks up. She makes a weepy little squeak. "M-My lady?"

Jay's freckles stand out against his cheeks like dun-gray ghosts.

"I'm alive," I croak. "Ch-Chair."

My Chair is chewing on the dead hero's bare left foot. Gristle pops as the Chair rips off a pair of toes. It swallows and oozes its way to me; Kestrel helps me climb into it. The Chair, sensing the aches grinding through my bones, softens its seat. Magical heat warms along my back.

"Good m-monster," I mumble, patting one of its arms.

I blink a little dazedly when Crane and Jay rush to me. Crane grabs my hand and cries on it. Jay *hugs* me.

"O-Okay," I say. "Stop that. Off. G-Get off. What the fuck."

I get it. Sort of. They're former Chosen Ones sent by the Portalis gods to drag me back to the temple. I saved them from the gods' betrayal, from being thrown back to Earth. That's the reason they work for me, why they stay—my anchor-spell is the only thing keeping everyone in the castle and surrounding lands from being uprooted and flung through a Door back to the mundane World of our birth.

The gods don't reward loyalty, I'd said.

True enough; the gods don't…but *I* do. Apparently, my people do, too.

Still…

"Stop h-hug, hug…*touching* me."

It's too much, with the clack-throb of my bones and my head pounding and dizziness creeping at the edges of my awareness.

They back off. Crane scrubs her face with a fist. "I'm sorry I killed him, my lady."

"Meh. We'll g-get another one at some, some— *later.* Just don't m-m-make it a habit. We need, need those."

Speaking of needs…I look to my consort. She understands immediately.

"Jay, draw another hot bath for the lady, please." I'm going to need to soak for a while or tomorrow will be a *nightmare.*

"At once, Lady Kestrel."

Kestrel and I look at the mangled meat oozing on my floor that used to be a Chosen One as Jay rushes to obey her. She sighs.

"This one almost saw the truth. What a pity."

My voice is so cold it burns my mouth. "Almost doesn't c-count for shit."

I'd always thought being betrayed would feel like someone punching me in the face. It didn't. Instead, the treachery slid between my ribs like a spike of ice lodging in my heart.

"It's time to go home. You have your own world to return to."

Truth. The Shadowlord, the monster I'd trained since I was seven years old to kill, had been telling the truth.

"But" despising how young my voice sounded, like the child I wasn't anymore, *"but Portalis is my home! I belong here. You* said—"

Nothing I said convinced the gods or their council of priestesses. They had called me through a Door, taken me into their temple, trained me. Raised me for a purpose, claiming to love me.

And all this time, they'd been lying to me, using me to get rid of the Shadowlord. Lying about what would happen once I was used up and useless.

Only Rook had told me the truth.

When I slipped into his cell the night before we were both to be sent back, he glanced up, a sneer twisting his face. But after one long look at my expression, the sneer melted into a detestable mix of sympathy and resignation.

"I told you so," gentle enough it somehow didn't slice open all the parts of me still raw from the gods' betrayal.

Words tangled together, glass shards in my throat. It hurt to swallow. I managed it somehow.

"Yeah, well…" I held up the key to his shackles. My voice ached with the salt of blood and tears. *"Fuck them. Right?"*

He smiled.

"What's your name, White Raven? Your real name?"

I had to laugh, wormwood and incredulity. "You're never going to believe this..."

Third time's the charm. Maybe all the sunshine and fluffy clouds are an auspicious sign. Maybe I should try to meet all the would-be heroes in my private garden instead of the forbidding, shadow-splashed great hall.

My Chair basks on a stretch of sun-warmed grass like some bizarre dog. Kestrel leans back against the silvery trunk of a tree, reading aloud while I pull weeds. Any of my people can do this for me—we have servants—but I enjoy the sun on the back of my neck, the soft breeze sweet with the perfume of midnight lilies, the quick snag of resistance before the weeds rip out of the dark soil.

Behind me, Shadowlord Rook clears his throat. I turn to him...and freeze. Kestrel slowly sets her book on the grass.

I swallow a laugh. Short, stocky Rook standing in my private garden, a pair of carrot-haired, freckle-spattered tweens pressing the points of their swords to his back and throat? He looks utterly mortified.

"What...happened." A demand, not a question.

"Caught this bastard in the privy," the tween boy says with pitiable triumph in his squeaky voice. "Didn't even have time to pull his pants up."

I grimace as Kestrel says, "Thanks for that image, brat."

"Now what?" I ask. I don't have a script for this, so I stick with short questions.

"Now you're going to surrender, Carrion Swan," the girl says. I wonder if they're twins or just sword-sibs, then decide I don't care. "Or we'll kill him."

"No," I say flatly.

Both children blink at me. Apparently, they hadn't planned past this point. Whoopsie.

Rook grins. "I told you, little heroes. The Carrion Swan can't be blackmailed."

If we were alone, I'd chastise him for lying to potential recruits. I can absolutely be blackmailed, unfortunately. Even cold-hearted, soulless killers have their soft spots.

Rook has *one* soft spot. Only one. And I've made sure that nobody has ever been able to use me against him.

I can't let it be known that *he* can be used against *me*.

"Do you want to go home?"

Time for the same old song and dance. The only reason I don't smash my own head in, is that every so often, a little hero-fish nibbles on my hook and

I get a new traitor to sign on with us. It's been so long though, I'm tired of this.

"Shut up," I say after the expected spiel about my wicked ways. My eyes never leave the steel point pressed against the line where Rook's grizzled beard meets his brown throat. The glint of metal, the quick bob of his Adam's apple, frazzles my voice into a stutter. "If you d-don't want to go back t-to Earth, if you want to…to stay *here*, put d-down your weap-weap…*swords*."

"No!" The boy yells. The girl stays quiet. A watchful little mouse to the boy's snapping dog. "We have our duty! The gods have ordered us to put an end to your murderous rampage."

"Rampage?" Kestrel squawks. "We're minding our own business! If you all would stop *coming* here—"

I lay a hand on her knee. My eyes are on the girl. Same carroty hair as the boy, but she's darker, and her eyes are brown instead of blue. Fewer freckles. Something about the way she moves with him says *not* siblings. Are they even friends?

"You torture people," she says at last. The other hero shoots her a poisonous look, as if she isn't supposed to speak. Rude. "We saw the corpses hanging from the gate. Your moat is full of mutilated bodies. You're not doing that in self-defense."

I've perfected the art of the elegant one-shoulder shrug.

"True enough. We don't go looking for trouble, but once it arrives…yes. We wring every drop of pain we can from the fools who invade my lands. What would you do to keep from being sent back to Earth?" I haven't gotten this far in the script in a long while, but my voice stays steady. "This place is your home, yes? What would you do to keep it?"

The boy hesitates. Not the girl.

"Anything."

A shadow flickers across the boy-hero's face. He didn't expect her to say that. One little fishy on the hook, perhaps?

"Anything. Then," my voice cool, almost indifferent, "can you blame me for doing exactly what you'd do in my place?"

"You murdered the greatest of the White Ravens," the boy says. I have to fight not to roll my eyes. "When you invaded the temple and freed the Shadowlord, you killed her, too. The one the gods named the Ravens for, you killed her!"

I smirk, just a little.

"Didn't, actually."

"Then where is she?" He demands. "Where is the Lady Raven, the First of the White Ravens, if you didn't kill her? Everyone knows you did!"

"Reports of my death have been greatly exaggerated." With a casual hand, I yank my hair ribbon so that my thick, natural curls spring free as I slowly stand. I have to be careful. Have to time this right, or in about five minutes I'm going to fall down *very* hard. And won't that be embarrassing? "Did it n-never occur to any of you I wasn't m-murdered? I ran away."

"That's stupid," says the boy. "Why would a Chosen One run away?"

"Maybe because we didn't feel like being dumped back on Earth like unwanted dogs," Kestrel says. "They bring us here, turn us into weapons, and once we do their bidding, they want to get rid of us?"

"You're making that up," the girl says. Her voice wobbles like a teardrop.

"What's your name?"

The boy snaps at me to mind my own business, but the girl says, "The temple named me Dove. But…but my name is Shrike."

Twice the venom in the boy's second vicious look. Not friends, these two. Not even sword-sworn allies.

"Shrike. Can you," I ask, enunciating very carefully, "think of a single story about a Door, and a Chosen One, and a Quest, where the Chosen One was allowed to stay when everything was all over, Shrike? Dorothy, Alice, Milo, Clara, Wendy. Even the Pevensies weren't allowed to stay forever. When have we ever been allowed a home to keep?"

There's a trick to this whole thing. Whether they get this far is a fifty-fifty shot, depending on the day of the week and the phases of the three moons and whether it's going to rain cherry-flavored lightdrops that evening and if I'm able to keep my inefficient blood from working against me…but once we get *here*, when I'm allowed to tell the truth—I ran away from the gods and became the villain on purpose—the new heroes always *know* it for truth.

It's a gift the gods forgot to steal back from me when I ran.

"Why…would they lie?" Shrike's voice cracks.

I sigh, just a little sorry for her. "Gods get bored. When they get bored, they play with us, until they're bored of that, too."

"Dove," the boy snarls, and Shrike flinches at the sound of her un-name. "Don't listen to her! It doesn't matter if they're going to send us back! She's evil and we have to kill or capture—"

But Shrike steps back, lowering her sword from Rook's throat. The poor kid's shaking her head, tears welling up in those big brown eyes.

"They lied to us."

"Dove—"

"That's not my name!" She looks to me. Her eyes burn, familiar desperation. "Don't let them send me back."

Before I can make my promise, the nameless hero launches himself at Shrike with a shout of "Traitor!"

And Rook, who has only one soft spot—betrayed hero-children whose hearts are broken by lies, who just want a safe place to call home—shoves himself between the furious Chosen One's sword and Shrike's shock-frozen body.

The temple really isn't sending their best, because the stripling barely manages to slice a shallow line across Rook's upper arm before my mentor thumps the brat on the head with a ham-sized fist and sends him sprawling.

I stare at the line of dark wetness staining Rook's gray sleeve, seeping into the lamb's wool robe I gave him last year for his birthday. My face tingles, the skin tight over my cheeks and temples. There's a roaring in my ears.

I slowly turn to look at the boy struggling to get off the grass. Twelve years old, perhaps. Old enough to understand what death is, yes? I should think so.

It doesn't matter if they're going to send us back.

Well enough, then.

"Rook," I say softly. "T-Take Shrike to, to the others."

It says more than either child might realize, that Shrike doesn't even turn to glance at the boy she arrived with, as the man who's like a father to me guides her inside to meet the rest of my people and see her settled in the castle.

"Chair!"

At my call, my Chair crawls to me on its thick, muscular tentacles and I sink gratefully into it. A fist squeezes my chest; I can breathe, but there's not enough air. It's not just the situation. I need to be horizontal.

Reading my thought, the Chair morphs, lengthening so I can pull my legs onto it and drop onto my back. The gray in my vision starts to fade.

"Shall I take that one to the lab, my lady?" Kestrel's voice thrums like a taut bowstring, each word a poison-tipped arrow.

"Yes."

I'm going to feed him to my spell…after I make him pay for hurting Rook.

⟶⟶⟩⟨⟩⟨⟨⟶

The first time I killed a temple soldier was to save Rook's life as we crossed the sanctified border into the forest. A girl I'd grown up with, trained with, been friends with. My blade burst through her chest and out her back as she swung her sword toward Rook's unprotected side.

The air stank of rust and viscera. I tasted metallic wetness on my lips.

We left her body in the dirt and ran through the night.

Rook stole horses for us. Rook chose our path. Rook did everything, while I bit my lip until blood ran and tried to keep my vision clear of tears.

Only at dawn did we make camp at the foot of the mountains. Rook tied up our horses. Rook got the fire going. Rook tended my injuries from the border skirmish.

And Rook was the one who sat beside me and held me as I finally broke and cried.

⋯⋯⋯

"Am I interrupting your brooding, little bird?" Rook has the same smile he had in the garden when he approaches me in my laboratory. I'm lounging in the Chair in front of a tall window, sipping idly from a glass of pink-stained wine. Anyone who didn't know me would assume it's a rosé. Anyone who dared steal a taste would learn better after the first fruit-and-rust mouthful.

"I d-d-don't brood," with a smile and a quirk of brows. "Just th-thinking about the, the state of our sp-spell supplies."

"You know," he says, flicking an apathetic glance at the observation window, "if you don't torture him, he'll last longer."

"H-He *deserves* it." My voice is like wolf teeth biting into the flesh of the words.

Rook doesn't torture. He'll kill, but he does it quickly.

He is far kinder than I am.

On the other side of the glass, the latest Chosen One, the boy who refused to bend, screams under Kestrel's knives. I shiver, the *rightness* of that scream prickling across my nape and fluttering in my chest.

It's evening, and he's strapped to a metal table in a special room in my lab, lit with blazing sunstones embedded in the white marble walls, and my beautiful Kestrel has him under her blood-slick talons.

"How's y-your shoulder?"

"Doctor patched me up. Don't worry so much, kiddo."

Rook has just come from Sparrow, my best healer. I reward loyalty in my people.

Another long, shivering, perfect scream.

I sip the white wine, stained pink with the wretched hero's blood.

"H-How's Shrike set, set, settling in?"

"Seems okay. I gave her over to Crane and Jay."

"Good."

A beat of silence, and then, "After this, he may change his mind about not wanting to go back."

"Good f-for him." Even if I asked the brat now, while he writhed and screamed under the deft flensing of Kestrel's butchering knives, even if he gave the wrong-right answer now, I'd still shove him into my anchor-spell and drain every last drop of life and soul from his scrawny body when my love finished with him.

Hurt my family and suffer.

"Another one is coming to our door right now," Rook says.

I raise an eyebrow. "A third, third—*three* heroes?"

"Appears to be. Shrike says this one is a favorite of the boy's."

Indeed?

I drain my wineglass in a few quick swallows, then tap the spell-circle inscribed in the window. When I speak, Kestrel hears me. So does the hero.

"Seems our f-friend had some back, back—reinforcements. Shall w-w-we unroll the, the welcome m-mat, my love?"

Under all the blood and grit, the Chosen One's eyes snap open. He stares at me through the glass.

"Please," a scratchy, mousy sound from a raw throat. "Please…don't hurt her."

I just look at him.

Only luck put Rook in the path of his pathetic attempt at hostage-taking instead of Kestrel. Only luck spilled Rook's blood. If this whelp had scratched my Kestrel…I love Rook, but if it had been my consort bleeding in the garden, I'd be flaying this would-be hero myself, rather than watching him ooze and whimper while my Kestrel drags a blade from the dip of his collarbone over his skinny chest.

Fresh tears spill down his cheeks, leaving tracks in the red.

He's not crying about the new wound.

I smile and tap the arm of my Chair. It rises on squamous tentacles and carries me away from the observation window to my throne room to prepare for my next guest.

The gods will learn eventually—I promised I'd do anything to keep from being sent back. And I keep my promises.

Bloodlust

Gnosis

I never thought I'd be old. I never wanted to be. Now, I never will be.

GNOSIS

I woke up in darkness. The air around me was scarce and damp. I couldn't move. It was when I tasted dirt that I knew I was buried. How? It all came flooding back to me. I was dead. I went on a date the night before. It was a first date, I met her briefly before, but I didn't know her. I rarely date, but I gave it a shot because it had been a while, and she was gorgeous. I did not expect the night to end with me going back to her place. I hate sleeping anywhere but my bed. I did not expect to see fangs extrude from her incisors while we were kissing on her sofa. I really didn't expect her to bite the soft part of my neck and drink my blood slowly from my veins. Sure, it was hot, but I did not sign up for this.

The panic set in as I realized what happened. I was claustrophobic and needed to get out of this coffin in the ground. I racked my brain for anything I knew about vampires. I guess I was becoming one. First step, get out of here. At least the mortician had the decency to bury me with my nice cane. I could barely move, but I managed to slide my cane into my hands and start pounding on the lid of the coffin. I didn't have much space, but I was determined. I continued knocking the skull shaped handle of my cane into the wood of the coffin lid until there was a satisfying crack. I smiled to myself. Finally, I've gotten somewhere.

I began to push on the lid with my hands and struggled under the weight of the lid and the dirt. In life, I was not strong, although my physical therapist kept me functioning for the most part. In death, with vampire strength starting to set in, I was able to push the coffin lid off. Dirt came pouring in quickly. I tried to move as the dirt came crashing down on top of me. Strength was foreign to me, but I could feel my body resisting the dirt pouring on top of me. I was able to sit up. This vampire strength was no joke. I moved my cane to position it against the bottom of the coffin and the dirt began to fill in where my body laid moments before. Slowly, carefully and with my head down so as not to get dirt in my eyes, I began to stand. I raised an arm above my head and pushed through the dirt until I felt the cool night air on my fingers as my hand rose from the grave like in horror movies. Freedom at last.

I never thought I'd live forever. I thought that I would die young as many of us do. I had hoped so. If I lived with crippling pain that worsened through the years, I didn't want many years. I knew what I needed to do. I needed to find my hot date, Amy, and drink her blood. I knew it was the next step in the process. Then, I'd have to kill her.

GNOSIS

As I pulled myself from the grave I was buried in, I took a look at my surroundings. I'd lived in this small, southern town for much of my life and immediately recognized the building attached to the cemetery as the Catholic church I went to when I was in Catholic school. I had long left the Catholics behind in search of a better god, but I never found one.

I dusted off my black clothes to remove the dirt from myself and began to walk. I knew where Amy lived, I had been there the previous night. I needed to make a quick stop outside the church. I knew I couldn't go in, now that I was damned, but I didn't need to. I walked over to the crucifix outside of the church. It burned me, but I didn't care. I looked at Jesus' crucified body. I stared at his face. If there ever was a god, he had long since abandoned me.

I hadn't been able to walk a mile for years. I tired quickly and could only walk about a quarter of a mile with a cane at a time. Sometimes less. Some days I used a wheelchair to get around, but in my current housing situation that wasn't an option. Now, I was walking much faster than I had in years. I was making quick progress back towards the heart of the town. Back towards where Amy lived. I began to feel nervous. What was I thinking, just showing up there? What if she didn't mean to turn me? I didn't see any other option, and it didn't matter. What should have taken me forty minutes to walk, I was there in twenty. I found myself in front of Amy's door. I took a deep breath, one that I didn't really need now that I was a vampire, and knocked on her door.

She answered quickly, looking a bit disheveled but still gorgeous. Her pink, curly hair was tousled, and her colorful dress was slipping off her shoulder.

"Amy," I said, "Good to see you."

Why was I trying to make small talk?

"Zagan? What have you been up to?" She seemed amused. I was getting annoyed.

"Well, I just crawled out of my own grave, and I just had to see you. I'm not sure how I got there." I said dramatically, "The last thing I remember is our date last night. My memory is a bit fuzzy, but I think it ended with you sinking your fangs into my neck." Amy still looked amused.

"Just come in," she reached out to pull me by the arm into her apartment.

I looked around me. Everything was the same as it had been the night before. Amy's pink hair, her home decor featuring elegant red and black hues, mixed with silver and rainbows, was all exactly as I remembered it. Pentagrams, jack-o-lanterns, bats and drawings of naked women filled her home. She didn't care much for overhead lights and preferred to light the room with candles. Maybe that's what drew me to her. I could never resist a girl with a love of the macabre.

Amy noticed me looking around.

"Sit down, would you?" She was growing impatient.

She laid on the purple chaise longue in her living room and poured herself a drink that looked like red wine from a dark bottle. I realized quickly that she was drinking blood. It left me feeling queasy at first, but I realized I needed to get used to the idea of drinking blood quickly. I sat next to her. I couldn't help but notice how full her lips looked as she sipped slowly from her glass.

"I know what you did to me. I don't know why you did it, but I know enough to know what comes next." I said, trying to be confident.

"And what would that be?" She looked at me, eyes cast downward as she took another sip of her drink.

I was really starting to get pissed.

"I need to drink your blood," I said flatly. "I've read enough to know that's the final step in vampiric transformation." Amy looked amused.

"I'll let you drink my blood, love. If you make it worth my while." I was confused. She must have noticed. "Let's pick up where we left off last night." Amy slid closer to me, her dress falling further from her shoulder. If I still needed to breathe, my breath would have hitched.

I knew what she wanted. She glared at me with bedroom eyes. I was fucking furious. If she hadn't turned me, maybe sex would still be on the table. I had been completely content living a mortal life and dying a mortal death. I had no desire to be immortal. Killing people and drinking their blood was really neither here nor there, but I couldn't stand the idea of immortality. I needed a way out. There is so much lore about how to kill a vampire. I just needed to find a way to make sure one would stay dead. My mind was racing with ideas.

"We hardly know each other." I said, "Isn't that sort of thing usually saved for the third date?" I mused.

Amy rolled her eyes.

"I could wait an eternity," she took another sip from her glass, "but who says I have to wait for you? I could get anyone I want."

She looked pleased with herself and sipped again. She was right.

She was an ethereal being, and she looked it. Damn. I knew I'd have to keep her interested in me if I was going to get what I wanted. I needed her blood, and a bit more time to figure out what I was going to do.

"Tell you what, why don't we go on another date? The night is young, and I'd love to know more about you. We can see where the night takes us."

Amy smiled. It was a beautiful and terrifying sight, really.

"I accept," she said, "on one condition. You can't go out in those dirty clothes. You can borrow something of mine!"

She was excited now. I grimaced. I doubted her colorful wardrobe would have anything I would feel comfortable wearing, but I agreed.

Amy's closet contained all the colors of the rainbow. I immediately started looking at the darker end of the spectrum. I tended to dress in black and darker hues, but Amy's wardrobe was all over the place. After saying no to several dresses Amy pulled for me, I settled on a purple, strappy pentagram tank and black skinny jeans. I kept my black combat boots and gave them a bit of a wash in the sink to get more of the dirt off. I looked in the mirror to inspect my reflection, which of course, wasn't there. That was something I would have to get used to. I let Amy adjust my facial jewelry to get the caked dirt out of it. She fixed my spiky black hair for me with some hairspray, and we were ready to go.

"You look great," Amy said, "Just think of how much time you'll save doing makeup with the new pallor of your skin," she winked.

Amy decided we were going to a shitty club downtown. It wasn't my scene. Clubs never had enough seating, and they were too loud, but I went along with it.

***

When we arrived at the club, the music was already too loud. The rainbow lights were bright and the night was dark. Amy whispered something to the bouncer and giggled, and we got in without paying.

"What did you say to him?" I asked as she dragged me by the arm into a sea of people. "Just a little hypnosis," she replied. "Don't worry about it. Let's dance!"

I wasn't usually much for dancing, especially without a drink or two in me.

"I want a drink," I told her.

"You can't have human libations, silly," she giggled again, "at least not directly." Amy pulled me close. "You'll have to drink the blood of drunk humans to get a buzz," she practically yelled in my ear, "and oh, you can't do that until you're a full vampire, so I guess you're out of luck."

She snickered and licked my ear for good measure. I shuddered with delight. Maybe this wouldn't be so bad.

We danced for hours without getting tired. Amy was intoxicating all on her own. The way she bumped and grinded with me left me in a trance. Eventually, she got bored. She grabbed my face and pulled me close.

"Take me home," she looked up at me and bit her lip before pulling me into a kiss.

Steadying myself on my cane, I reached up to touch her face with my free hand, deepening the kiss. She pulled away and looked at me, lips ruddy.

"Anything you want," I said to her. And I actually meant it. This was going to be harder than I thought.

We left the club giddy and sweaty from dancing. Amy grabbed my hand as we walked back to her place. I couldn't believe the amount of physical activity I had participated in today. Sure, my knees ached, and my body begged me to lay down, but much less than usual.

"I have a question for you," I rubbed my thumb over her hand, "why did you turn me?" I practically begged for an answer.

"Don't know," she replied, "in my hundreds of years on this planet, I haven't felt the way I felt when we kissed last night. It was electric." she looked up at me and bit her lip again, "I've turned so many vampires, but I thought you and I could really have some fun together. It was a spur of the moment decision, really."

Hundreds of years? Have some fun? My life, and death, were not to be toyed with. I was starting to get angry again, but I couldn't deny the connection I felt with her. This was going to be harder than I thought.

We reached her apartment and Amy unlocked the door. She made a grand gesture of holding it for me, but I knew I had to wait to be invited in. She giggled.

"That was a test. Look at you following the rules. You'll make a better vampire than I thought."

I felt a pang of disgust. Amy waltzed into her apartment and stuck out her hand to me.

"Come," she demanded. I took it.

GNOSIS

I propped my cane by the door. She led me to her bedroom. The walls were a royal purple and decorated with more art of nude women. I can't lie, I really liked the vibe. A queen-sized bed with black satin sheets sat to the right of the room. To the left, a plush lined coffin. I gulped. This was getting real. Amy bounced onto the bed and patted beside her, motioning for me to sit. If my heart still beat, it would be racing. She turned towards me and batted her eyelashes. I knew she wanted me to kiss her. I wanted to. I knew I'd have to in order for her to let me drink her blood. I needed full vampiric strength to do what needed to be done. I tucked her hair behind her ear and touched the soft skin of her face. I pulled her towards me and kissed her.

It felt different than it had the night before, and even in the club. It was more intense than any kiss I had in life. I felt sparks fly. Amy reached around me to pull me closer. I could imagine how heavily I'd be breathing if there was air in my lungs. She pushed me onto the bed. She was so strong. She climbed on top of me and pinned my arms above my head. I might have let a small whimper escape. Amy snarled at me, satisfied with her work so far. My eyes widened. She sat up straight and slowly caressed my face. I touched the soft skin of her forearm.

"Drink," she demanded. I was surprised.

"But…" I started.

"Don't argue, just do it. It's more fun that way." She winked at me.

I was ravenous. I was ready to claim my full power. I just wasn't ready to part with her yet. I brought her arm to my face. I felt a hunger I had never felt before. I felt a sharp pain in my mouth as fangs extended from my canines for the first time. I looked up at her, and she nodded encouragingly. I bit into her soft skin and sucked the blood from her lifeless veins.

Amy cried out in pleasure as I drank her blood. The sensation was unlike anything I had ever experienced before. I sucked and gulped and moaned.

"That's enough," she said. "Don't be greedy."

I released my jaw from her arm, blood dripping down my face and throat, ruining my borrowed clothes. I looked up at her. She smiled and stroked my face.

"You look perfect," she said, "with blood on your face. Like you were meant for this."

Before I could get angry again, I felt intense pain all over my body. I'd lived with chronic pain for years, but this was far worse. I cried out and curled into the fetal position, shaking and closing my eyes.

"Shhh," Amy said, stroking my hair, "Your transformation is almost complete." she giggled.

The pain began to subside, and I opened my eyes to look at her with sharper vision than I'd ever had as a human. The world around me looked crisper and clearer than it ever had, even with my contact lenses.

I slowly unfurled myself from the fetal position and sat up. I took inventory of my body, something I practiced when I was alive. No pain anywhere. Usually, my joints were stiff and aching. I ran my hands along my skin and noticed my scars from various surgeries were fading and then gone entirely. Amy looked at me, expectantly. I assume the other vampires she had turned must have been grateful for altering their bodies in this way. I was angry. Of course, I didn't like to be in pain most of the time, physical or mental, but sometimes it was enough to remind me that I was human. On the worst days, when I couldn't get out of bed and didn't feel like a person, I was reminded that I was. I was not grateful for the pain that comes with being a human, but she took my humanity. She took my ability to feel the sunlight, and to enjoy food and drink and desserts. God, I loved desserts. She took the beating of my heart, the breath from my lungs, the warmth from my skin. I was furious. My plan. I had to remember my plan.

I kissed Amy roughly, smearing her own blood on her face with mine. I practically growled at her as I pushed her down onto the bloodstained sheets. We went on like this for a while. Kissing, with our faces covered in blood. Sharp fangs and inhuman noises came from both of us. It was a power struggle, really, with both of us fighting for dominance. Amy slid her hands down my body, and I shuddered. It was time. I stopped her with my own hands.

"Let me get freshened up first," I gave her a quick kiss and slithered out of bed.

"Don't be long!" she whined after me.

I walked through Amy's apartment, taking in the tastefully pornographic art one more time. I didn't know what would happen to me if I went through with my plan. I could easily, and quickly, become the most hated vampire for killing one of my own. If other vampires even knew about me yet, surely, they would hunt me down and kill me. The alternative was that I would die, too, since Amy had turned me. I would also kill all the other vampires she had turned.

"Good," I thought to myself, "I'll take as many of them out as I can."

I had finally settled on how I was going to do it. I stopped in the bathroom to wash my face of Amy's blood, although it was all over me at that point. With no reflection, I was never going to be able to get it all off anyway. After a few minutes of scrubbing, I continued down the hallway to the entrance, where I had left my cane. I eyed it carefully. I picked it up by the decorative skull handle and twisted it slowly to reveal the hidden blade inside. I would have taken a deep breath if I still could. I replaced the handle loosely and slowly walked back to Amy's bedroom.

Amy had taken the liberty of removing her bloodstained clothes. She laid in a very sultry position, covering herself loosely with the satin sheets. I leaned against the doorway to take in the sight. I noted every curve where the sheet clung to her body.

"Come here," she whispered.

I obeyed. I sat at the edge of my bed, keeping my cane in my hands. Amy came up behind me, letting the sheet fall. She touched my neck, fingers lingering over the mark she had made last night. I winced, not from pain, but from the memory. Her hands traced my collarbones and shoulders.

She leaned down to whisper "Let me take your clothes off."

I nodded. I was always weak in the knees, but especially when a woman said that to me. She gracefully took my borrowed top off and ran her hands down the sides of my body, over my binder. I leaned into her touch but did my best to stay alert. When she reached my hips, I stiffened. She must have noticed.

"What?" she stopped.

I turned on her then.

I quickly pulled the blade from my cane and whipped around to face her. With my cane in the other hand, I pushed the two together to form a cross and pushed them at her as she scrambled away from me, looking hurt.

"What do you think you're doing?" she demanded.

"You played with my life and death. Now it's my turn," I replied bitterly.

"You're making a mistake," she hissed, "I'm stronger than you. I know how to use my strength."

She was right. I didn't know how I was going to do this; I just knew it had to be done.

"Doesn't matter," I growled, "your time is up, bitch."

I threw myself at her, blade first. She grabbed the blade with her hand, cutting her skin, and laughed as the fresh blood trickled down. I was quicker now that I was a full vampire. I used my other arm to swing the rest of the wooden cane at her, connecting it with her skull. It made a satisfying crack and she groaned gutturally.

"Now you're pissing me off," she said.

The wound on her hand was already healing and she rubbed the dent out of her skull. She rose from the bed and extended her fangs, snarling at me. She hissed and came towards me full force. I slashed at her, nicking her face a few times. She caught my wrist and snapped it with little effort. I screamed and she laughed wickedly. I brought my cane to the floor and used it to steady myself as my bones began to mend. I couldn't yet use that hand to wield my weapon, so I lashed at her knees with my cane. She wasn't expecting that. I heard more bones crack as she fell to the floor. I ran behind her and took her into a headlock, using my cane for leverage. My wrist wasn't fully healed, but this was my chance. I raised my blade and came down on her throat with such force that it took her head clean off. Without vampire strength and with a blade this small, I would never have achieved this. Blood spurted from where her throat was and she made a gurgling noise that I thought may have been laughter. Her body slumped to the floor and her head rolled in front of me. Her eyes were glassy, and her mouth was open in a snarling smile with her fangs showing. This was a truly horrifying sight. Amy's apartment was a mess. I didn't know if beheading her was enough to kill her. I needed to get out of there quickly.

I found garbage bags and lighter fluid under the sink in her kitchen and tossed her head into a garbage bag. I put my own dirty, but less bloody, clothes back on. I found matches next to Amy's many candles. All that was left to do was commit a bit of arson and get the hell out of there. I took the bag and my supplies and left Amy's apartment. I expect I should have felt remorse for what I did, but that hadn't set in yet. Maybe it never would. I was pretty unphased by the events of the evening. I walked to the dumpster in her apartment complex and tossed the bag in. I poured the lighter fluid in after. I struck the match on the side of the box and tossed it in. I lit a few more for good measure. Once I was sure it would light, I ran.

I ran for the first time in years. It was honestly delightful. I felt a breeze brush past my face as my body carried me much faster than it ever did when I was a human. I heard flames crackle behind me, and I kept running. After about a mile, all of a sudden, I felt a tightening sensation throughout my body. It became so intense that I stopped. I was gagging and choking. I doubled over and fell to the ground, as my own blood gurgled up out of my throat. I guess I was going to die by killing the vampire who turned me. I lay on the ground, unable to move as my surroundings faded. I realized where I was. I was back at the church yard and saw Jesus staring down at me. He looked like he was laughing. I let go and felt at peace. The sun began to rise.

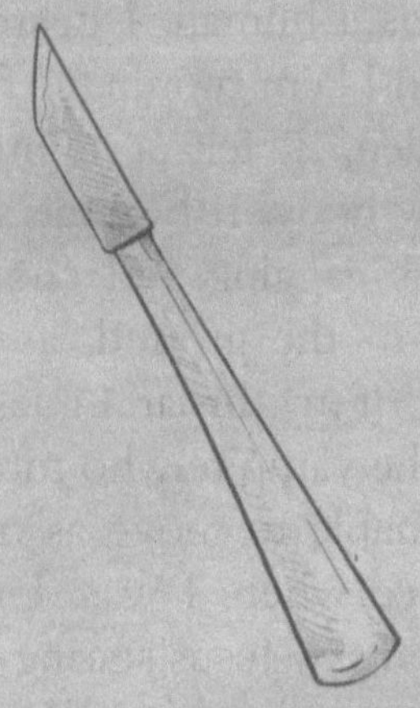

Bored Now
Shannon Massey

hen you've lived as long as I have trivial distinctions (good, bad, right, wrong) evaporate and life is all about what feels good and staves off the boredom.

Now I'm hunting for my next toy. Someone to ·play with and leave in a broken pile. Sometimes a broken pile of body parts, others just a pile of used tissues and self-esteem.

A recent toy made the mistake of saying I couldn't be a vampire (not what I am, but a word humans applied more than once) because of my missing pieces. Said vampires couldn't be imperfect. Oh, how she's suffered for having the audacity. People worshiped me as a god. Countless men and women have waxed poetic about my beauty. No one is as close to perfect as me.

Every time I pull her out of her box, she begs me to kill her. Every time I remind her of what she said and that she'll be paying for that mistake until she dies of old age. A lifetime of pain and torment is justified by her ableist nonsense.

While I'll fuck anyone, doesn't matter who or what you are, I prefer women. Soft skin, warm bodies, and they are so fun to manipulate and break. Men are easier to control, a few words to stroke their delicate egos and they're putty in my hands. Some of the most horrific atrocities to befall humankind were because I was bored and knew how to twist men's insecurities and desperation for power.

Tonight, I just want to fuck someone senseless and feed. Someone that could fight me, who exudes strength and power but wants to submit. Pulsing lights flash and what they call music reverberates through my chest as bodies grind against each other. The delightful scent of sweat, arousal, and pheromones floats around the dancefloor.

"Daddy looked like that when we was hunting," someone drawls from the stool to my right. "Are you a hunter?"

I have to turn; I never had a right eye. A small curvy blonde sits perched there wide eyed. She's so—ordinary. Literally, nothing stands out or draws attention to her. I don't know if she's even worth the time I took to turn to her. "Excuse me?" I ask, adjusting my eyepatch slightly. Humans are squeamish if I don't cover up.

Her cheeks blush, and breath quickens when I fix her with a stony glare. "Uh, I asked if you're a hunter," she murmurs. "Gosh, you're pretty. Never seen someone so pretty as you." She blushes deeper and brushes her hair behind her ears. "Um, I never been to one of these places before. I'm, uh, I'm Mabel."

Oh, she is too easy, a gazelle stumbling into a lion's den. "Mabel," her name feels good in my mouth, I bet the rest of her would too. "You've never been to a bar?" I ask, teasing.

She shrugs, fidgeting with her cocktail napkin. "A gay one," she whispers, as if the words may

bite. "I… I'm gay, I think? But don't really know—
"

Strong prey can wait, an easy snack will be fun. I lean down and kiss her. Some people ask but I take what I want, and she is going to give me everything I need.

"Oh wow, yeah, I'm definitely gay," she murmurs breathlessly when I break the kiss. "Never kissed no one before. You're good at that."

"Well then, it looks like I was hunting you, Mabel," I say with a wicked smile.

She blushes and sputters. This is going to be easier than I expected.

Kissing her again as my hands slide down her wide, supple hips, hooking under her full ass and picking her up off her barstool so I can slide under and sit her in my lap. Grateful, I switched into this prosthetic before leaving my gallery. Technology is a wonderful thing; I can feel the heat radiating off her. Mabel may not be a pet or toy, just a fun way to waste a few hours. I kiss over and nibble her earlobe as my hand discreetly moves up her trembling leg. "We can do this here, or I can take you home."

She nods, completely incapable of speaking and whimpers.

"Say something. Should I continue here, or take you home?"

"Please?" she pushes out, leaning down to kiss me. Fear, anticipation, panic, pleasure, she's feeling so many things it's hard to sort them all out.

I smile and kiss her again. "Please what, my little doe," I murmur against her lips.

"Please take me home," she whispers.

I stand, taking her with me.

"I can walk," she says breathlessly. She may come undone just from kissing, which is always fun to provoke.

"Not for long," I respond, biting her lip.

She whimpers, eagerly kissing back, arms tentatively wrapping around my neck.

"Never done this before, neither," she says. "Daddy taught me not to go home with strangers. Mama told me I gotta wait for my wedding night. Be pure 'til I can be my husband's."

How quaint. Who should I be today... She's drinking a martini, or not drinking, it's sitting in front of her, untouched. "I'm Olive," I whisper in her ear. "Now we're not strangers."

I'm almost out the door when a scarred hand lands on my shoulder, and I'm spun around. The only person stupid enough to do that is the one person I was sure I'd never see again. Well, she runs away but always ends up back. Either I catch her, or she crawls back. I broke her centuries ago and she doesn't know how to be broken with anyone else.

"Put her down and back away," Little Shadow snarls in a long-forgotten language, rainbow-colored nails biting into the skin of my shoulder.

Oh, she's regained her strength, which means I get to break her again. The thought excites me. I'll have strong prey and weak prey. I get a whiff of something else, a Hunter, I don't see her but she's close.

"Hello, Little Shadow," I respond with a smile and reach up to brush at the curls of the wig she's wearing. "This is consensual, isn't it, my little doe?" I add in English. Maybe in the time she's been away she's had time to learn more than please stop, Master.

Mabel nods, looking from me to my shadow. "She's so pretty and her lips are real soft. I'm okay, miss, promise."

Oh, now she's really tempting fate. Little Shadow leans in and kisses my prey, then almost as an afterthought me. "I'm going to kill you, asshole," she murmurs as she pulls away.

I catch her and hold her where she is. This prosthetic doesn't have the exciting attachments my other one does so I squeeze tighter, Little Shadow's right shoulder never heals properly. A flash of pain lights up her eyes.

"No, you won't. If you're a good girl and come home, I won't punish you for running," I respond, licking my lips.

"Oh, I didn't realize you's foreign; that sounds so pretty, whatever you two was speaking. Who is she?" Mabel whispers, cheeks blushing.

I smile and chuckle. "A soulmate, we're going to do beautiful things to you, my little doe."

"No, we're not," Little Shadow responds in accented English. But her resolve is already deteriorating, she's never been able to say no to me. Well, she learned what happens if she's stupid enough to say no to me might be more accurate.

"Come, I'll share promise." I kiss her then kiss Mabel.

I don't wait, don't have to, she'll come and as much as she objects, she'll do anything I want because she's just another one of my broken playthings.

I met her, destroyed her, then made her eternal, just like me.

"Did you drive?" I ask Mabel.

Mabel shakes her head. "Uber. Um, your place, or mine? I got fancy tea if you want to go to mine?"

How sweet. "No, we're going somewhere special." I slip into a cab; my shadow reluctantly follows. Where the club smelled like desire, the cab reeks of poor choices and cheap perfume.

The cabbie glances in the rearview mirror. "Where ya headed?"

"Four Central Tower," I respond.

The cabby nods and takes off, merging into traffic.

Little Shadow shudders. "Wait, no, don't," she murmurs and starts to open the door, someone's shouting for the cab to stop.

I kiss her and twist the spot that always gets her to submit. "Stop."

Tears well up, but she knows better than to cry before I've asked her to.

"Is she okay?" Mabel asks.

I kiss Mabel again, allowing a hand to slip under her floral skirt. "Don't worry, my little doe. You want to have fun, right?"

She nods and moans. "Oh, wow."

"Tell me you want me to hunt you down and ravish you."

"Please," she murmurs, trying to move closer to me. I lean over and kiss Little Shadow, silent tears trickle down her cheeks, I bagged two presents tonight.

⁌⊱⊰⊱❈⊰⊱⊰⁍

The cabbie barely gets us where we need to go, I decided not to wait and started my fun in the cab. Mabel is a puddle and as angry as it makes her, so is my shadow.

When we step out of the cab together, Little Shadow turns to run. I grab her right arm. "Don't be stupid, come play."

She shakes her head slightly, so I twist her shoulder, relishing the way her face twists with pain.

"Safeword?" I ask, twisting a little harder.

"Delphine," her wife's name. Funny, she still equates the name with safety when there was nothing safe or secure about the terrible things I did to them.

"Safeword?" I ask my little doe, extracting myself from her.

"Don't stop, please?" she begs.

"Safeword," I state.

"I don't know what that is. More, please?" How beautifully she begs.

"Not yet. Be patient and wait. A safeword is something you say if you want me to stop."

"I don't want you to but Pinocchio?"

A finger grazes up her thigh, and she whimpers, leaning against the wall of the elevator.

I laugh. "You really are new, aren't you?"

Mabel nods. "Tonight was my first kiss, even." Oh, the sweet naivety, the way she blushes and emotions well up.

"No, you can't do this to a virgin, Naveen," Little Shadow says in a blend of several languages, shaking herself out from under my spell again.

Mabel perks up like a rabbit catching the scent of a predator. "Aren't you Olive?"

I kiss her and let my hand drift again, distracting her. "Don't worry, my little doe, let's have fun."

When we walk into my gallery Mabel whimpers, pleas for mercy surround us. I switch from the prosthetic I wear out to the one I made myself, designed to play with pets and prey.

"Relax, some people want pain, others pleasure. If you're a good little doe, I won't have to punish you."

Mabel turns back towards the door. "No, thank you, I wanna go home."

Before she can run, I wrap my arm around her waist and pull her into my arms. "Trust me, you want to, everyone always wants to," I offer, kissing her.

Her tears wet my cheeks and I kiss her harder. "I love when women cry," I whisper, gently biting her lip.

"Please don't hurt me, I wanna go home, I want my mom," Mabel whimpers.

Oh, Mabel… I pick her up and whisk her through the door into the other part of the playroom. The door shuts and I can still hear the squeals for mercy, but she won't be able to. "Like I said, some people like pain, others want pleasure. Let me pleasure you, little doe."

She's still trembling and crying, casting my shadow a tearful glance. "Don't let her hurt me, please miss, I wanna go…"

"I won't." The conviction is adorable and so sincere.

I kiss my doe lightly and wipe her tears away. Continue kissing her as I walk her back towards the king-sized bed, clothes leaving a trail behind us. I look at my shadow. "Are you going to undress yourself, or do you need help?" I hope she needs help; I've missed the way she screams and begs.

Instead, she reluctantly starts undressing while shuffling towards the bed.

"Sweet baby Jesus, who did that to you?!" Mabel asks, eyes wide. I push her and she falls back on the bed with a startled gasp.

I look back, and Little Shadow has tears dripping down her cheeks. Her body was my canvas. I painted the entire thing, save her beautiful face with gentle flicks of my blade. Immortalizing the night we met, she screamed so sweetly before I gave her the eternal kiss.

"Naveen, I won't let you hurt her," she states, again such conviction.

"You will," I respond, grinning. "Now, my little doe, let's strap you down—"

"Pinocchio? Don't know if—" she bursts into tears and puts a hand across her bare chest.

While I'm cruel and don't always stop, I do honor safe words. So, I sit next to her and kiss the beautiful tears away. "Oh, Mabel, you asked if I was a hunter; I am and I caught you. Now I want to play, we'll have fun like in the cab."

With exciting sobs, Mabel brings knobby knees to her chest and wraps flabby arms around them. Such perfect prey. "Please don't hurt me! Mama said sinners bring on the devil. Don't want her to be right," she wails.

Well, now that just kills a mood. Can't very well let her die thinking she deserved this because of religious fools. Little Shadow releases a relieved breath, remembering that is the only way to get me to stop once I've set my mind to playing with you.

"While I am a demon, you have nothing to fear from me. No games, no strings, let me show you just how good this can feel. Let us." I turn and look at my shadow still standing there ready to attack. "Let's have a good night."

And with that, Little Shadow obediently comes to the bed and curls into me. "I like good nights," she murmurs.

With what I hope is a reassuring smile, I push out a deep breath. "How about it, Mabel?"

She looks at us. "Promise not to hurt me? Did you do that to her?"

I look down at my shadow and kiss her forehead, pulling off the wig she's wearing. "Sometimes I lose myself in beautiful moments and must immortalize them. Only a living canvas will suffice."

Mabel's eyes get wide. "Don't make me a canvas." Alligator tears drip down her cheeks and oh how I want to hear her scream.

Instead, I smile. "No, my little doe, I just want to fuck you senseless. Perhaps we both will?"

I see her shiver and she nods. "Don't hurt me, but please do what you were doing in the cab?" she whispers. "Felt awful good, never felt none of that before."

"The way you sound when you beg." I grin and lick my lips. "Lie back—please." The please added for Mabel and Little Shadow, I need them to relax and not question what's about to happen. Have fun here, then we'll go to the other room, and I'll have proper fun with Little Shadow.

Mabel nervously lies back on the silk pillows. "Wow, these are soft," she whispers, a hand floating up to play with the fabric of the pillowcase.

I look down at my shadow and kiss her gently. "Oh, my pet, I'm so glad you're home."

Little Shadow both loves and hates the fact she's lying here in my arm; I can see the internal struggle. "I was going to stay away this time."

I run my hand across the art on her scalp. "I know."

She bites her lip, eyes cast down. "But then I saw you tonight."

Little Shadow can run as many times as she wants, but always ends up back here. "I know."

"I hate you." The venom is there but the bite isn't.

I chuckle. "Yes, pet, I know."

"But I don't too." She chokes on those words, hates to say them out loud, but I always love to hear them.

"Lie next to each other; let's have some good wholesome fun."

—⟨⟩⟨⟩—

Little Shadow sobs frantically as I put her in her special place. "No! Said we'll have a good night, promised not to hurt her!"

Technically, that was yesterday since it's after midnight, so I gave them a good night. "That was yesterday. Today I'm bored and need to remind you what you are."

"No, I'm not your broken puppet anymore!" she snarls, fighting viciously against the restraints.

Breaking her again is always more fun when she gets some pieces back together. Every time she thinks it'll be different, she'll beat me, every single time she's mistaken.

I laugh as she fights, screams, and curses while I fix toys to her. All designed for maximum pain but minimal damage; I can't ruin my artwork. Some are oldies created for the inquisition or go back further to my childhood and how kings dealt with slaves and criminals, like me. I lost my hand when I was only six, taken for stealing something to eat. Lost so much more before Desdemona gave me the eternal kiss and taught me all about revenge. How good it can feel to inflict pain on others. To take pleasure in the screams for mercy. Eventually she outlived her usefulness, so surprised when she found herself on the other side of my blade.

I only stop playing with Little Shadow when Mabel staggers in, surprisingly, hands against her bloody throat.

"Olive, I don't feel good," she murmurs, staggering towards the door.

"Let me help you feel better, my little doe." Do what I did to Little Shadow. Another eternal plaything.

"No! Don't!" my shadow shouts as I move towards Mabel. "Don't! I'll let you use fire tools, make me a puppet or a pet, do anything! Just don't give her the same eternity I have. Please don't."

This is the first time in all our centuries together she's offered to sacrifice her sanity for someone else. Willingly giving me free range to do my worst, knowing just how horrific that can be.

"Really?" I shouldn't ask, I should take this gift, but I'm genuinely shocked.

"Yes, really, please don't. Please, I'm begging, I'll do anything."

I lick Mabel's neck. Tears trickle down her cheeks. "Was Mama right? Is this 'cause I'm a sinner?"

"No, my sweet little doe, not at all."

I go back to my shadow and kiss her, gently biting her lip. "Because I'm feeling generous, I won't take advantage of the gift you gave me. She's too good to waste, will be a blood bag instead."

"What? No! No, that's worse. Please let me save her; I need to save her!"

I smile wickedly. "Foolish little pet, you can't save anyone, not even yourself. Let me get her set up, then I'll be back to start your first session."

"No!" she screams, frantically pulling at the restraints again.

Being a predator surrounded by submissive prey is glorious; their fear crackles in the air like exposed wires.

I need to find a fresh canvas to immortalize this. So many beautiful works of art already bless the walls of my gallery.

In a dark forgotten corner I find the perfect new canvas, forgot I had her. Didn't like how I treated Little Shadow. Was going to stop me, I stopped her instead.

"Well now, I forgot about you, pet. You'll do nicely."

The canvas tries to fight me as I remove the restraints to move her to my easel.

I laugh. "How many times do we have this conversation, pet? There's nowhere *to* run."

I let her get out of my grip and watch the false hope fuel her.

She sees my new blood bag. I've decided she no longer has a name; I'm going to erase that from her. Break her because I can. If she wasn't so wonderful to play with, she could have gone home. Had a night to tell her friends or coworkers about, assuming she has those. Then the new canvas sees my shadow on her special spot.

"What the fuck?" she murmurs.

"Run," Little Shadow sobs, her special spot hurts in all the right places. Pain already eroding her resolve.

Instead of running, my new canvas turns and grabs one of my scalpels, perfect for detail work.

"No! Run!" Little Shadow begs.

"I won't let you hurt her anymore," the canvas shouts at me.

This is too much fun to pass up. Over my thousands of years so many have tried to kill me, no one has come close to succeeding. Well, that's a lie. Before the eternal kiss, several nearly succeeded; I repaid them in kind.

My canvas has trouble staying on her feet, we played a game when she first came to my gallery where I tried to break every bone in her legs. They mustn't have healed right, which means she's probably in a lot of pain right now. Yet she still needs to rescue the damsel.

"You're going to end up like my shadow, another canvas to paint and body to play with."

The canvas lunges again, I step away again; I smile and glance up at my shadow. "I'll move my easel so you can watch. It's going to take at least as long as you did."

Little Shadow's fighting again, trying to get off, which will just end up hurting her worse. How I missed the sweet scent of her blood; copper with floral backnotes, and she screams so beautifully. While I'm distracted, the canvas gets me in the side with the blade. Gets me three more times before I register she's attacking, over the excitement of witnessing Little Shadow falling to pieces again. Maybe I'll let the canvas think she's won? Be the hero, then make her watch as I punish my shadow, make my shadow watch as I paint my next masterpiece. They'll all watch and there will be nothing they can do to stop it.

I let her strike me one more time, then fall. She goes for my shadow first; I watch but lay motionless, I'm a walking corpse so it's not hard.

She limps to my shadow. "I'm gonna get you out, hang on,"

My shadow is sobbing, trying to wave the canvas away. "Won't stay died, never do, leave, run!" her English is as broken as she is.

Oh, this is too perfect. I almost want to laugh as she shakes her head. "Ain't leavin' you! Ended up here cause I wanted to help you, so I'm gonna help. How the fuck are you…? Oh Jesus, ok, I'm… just give me a minute, I'll get everything out and off."

The patience I have to lie and watch as she fumbles to get my shadow off her spot. They both go for the blood bag, she's more coherent and crying, such beautiful sounding tears.

"Don't wanna die, don't kill me!" she begs. "Mama and Daddy was right, sinners get paid in kind. I shouldn't've sinned, sorry I sinned—" she dissolves into tears.

Well, fuck, I can't let her die believing this is because of some warped interpretation of a text that wasn't translated properly. Or was translated in a way that helped sad, desperate men feel powerful. The same sad, desperate men I got to commit horrific atrocities in the name of their God.

My shadow shakes her head. "Won't. Am sorry she makes me hurt you!"

"Come on, we gotta get out of here!" the canvas shouts.

"Here! How escape last time."

I quietly count to ten before I go after them. "Should remember it takes more than a little stab wound to take me down, Little Shadow," I call out, taunting.

"Oh shit, run! Get her out!" the canvas says.

"Wants me. Take Mabel, run!"

Always love when she tries to be the savior, knowing it only makes everything worse. Centuries of the same pattern and same outcome and she still tries.

I laugh. "Be a good girl, go back to your perch, and I'll let them live. If you don't, I'll have to punish you all."

Little Shadow is sobbing harder. "Not going back."

I turn the corner, and they're trying to get out the door. I learned after Little Shadow's escape and installed extra locks. She stands in front of the other two and raises her fists. "I'm not going back, won't let you do that to me again," she snarls.

I smile. "You know how much I love when you fight back and give me a reason to punish you.

Come back with me, or I'll drag you back and punish you."

It's cute when they attack together, even cuter they think they can win. It's too easy to get my canvas and blood bag down. Little Shadow puts up a fight but I'm older and stronger, she doesn't stop fighting this time. Usually, she stops when she realizes she can't win but this time she keeps fighting, keeps getting up every time I knock her down.

"Oh, you really are asking for punishment now. I'm going to pull out all your favorite toys. Make you watch as I play with each of them, then it will be your turn. When I'm done with you, I'm going to start my next masterpiece."

She redoubles her efforts attacking with a renewed frenzy, I just start laughing harder. How I love when she fights like this, it's invigorating. Boredom staved off a little longer. It means it will take longer to break her. She almost does it this time, almost wins, but I get her pinned.

"I win, pet." I lean down and kiss her; she tries to bite me. "Oh, do I need to turn you into an actual pet again?"

Built a wonderful little box to keep her in. Only took her out when I was bored with other playmates and toys. After enough time she forgot how to talk, to behave, she was nothing but a snarling animal. The idea excites me.

"Yes, after I'm done with their punishment and yours, you'll go back in your box. Maybe this time you'll never get out."

The fight still burns in her eyes, but she's not going anywhere now I have her under me.

"She'll find me, promised you'd never hurt me again."

Now and then she finds someone that promises to save her from her evil lover. I always love when they inevitably fail because it's just one more person she gets to watch go to pieces.

"No one is going to swoop in and rescue you, Little Shadow." I pause for dramatic effect. "Though I always love when they try. Remember the last one? She tasted like strawberry wine and menthol cigarettes."

I pull her up and we walk back towards the gallery. She won't stop struggling and fighting. I have to take her to the ground and give her a fast, dirty session right there. This is disappointing, she's already squealing and begging to die. I pull her back to her feet, then reach down and grab the canvas by her hair and start moving back towards the gallery.

"Thora's going to kill you, promised. Said I could decide if it's fast or slow. Make you suffer.

Suffer like you've made me suffer," Little Shadow chokes out through beautiful sobs.

"No one is strong enough to take me," I remind her.

"A Hunter helped me, I love her," she responds.

Hilarious, a demon and her demon hunter. "Oh, I'm going to make you watch as I do wonderfully wicked things to her, make you do worse."

She fights again as I drag them down the hall and into the gallery. Fighting harder as I place her back on her special spot.

She screams and thrashes as I get my canvas on the easel.

I go back to the hallway, and Mabel is curled in a ball sobbing and praying. This isn't fun, this isn't what I want, this reminds me too much of things I want to forget. "Oh, Mabel, come here, my little doe," she fights me as I lean down and gather her in my arms, hugging her.

"Sinner, we sinned," she sobs. "Shoulda listened, married a man had babies spread the word," she sobs harder.

"No, pet, we didn't. Do you want to go home, or do you want to go back to bed? No punishment or pain, we can fuck all night and I'll take you to breakfast in the morning. Or you can go home right now."

"What about the others?" she asks; she's stopped trying to pull away and is curled into my chest.

Their pain will be endless because of the kindness I'm showing you, is what the inner voice is saying, as I'm rubbing her back and kissing her forehead. "I'm only offering this to you. Maybe they'll get their own deals?"

Without actually looking up, she glances up at me. "Wanna go home, you'll really let me?"

For now, then I'll hunt you down and have so much fun is the part I leave out as I nod and brush the hair from her face. "I'll take you home myself if that would help."

She takes a deep choppy breath. "No, thank you. I think I just want to go home and cry with my cat and ice cream."

Oh, Mabel, I undo the locks and open the back door. She doesn't think to go back and get her clothes or purse just runs down the dark dirt corridor sobbing. How I want to chase her and destroy her. Another time. Right now, I get to go play with Little Shadow, make her watch as I create another canvas.

A beautiful symphony of misery waits for me in the gallery.

I unroll my favorite tools and start working on my new canvas.

"Please stop, don't," my canvas begs.

"Long after you're gone, this will remain." I gesture at the canvases I've kept from over the years. This art form I've honed over millennia.

Oddly enough, the music of misery is settling.

"Oh, has someone wandered into my lair?"

Expanding my senses, I hear the heartbeats, smell the oil from the guns, almost taste the adrenaline. I walk up to my shadow, she's sniffing at the air, a smile curling her lips. "Told you, told you she'd come."

"And I promise you're going to watch her die. But I'm going to take my time and make her suffer."

They come in weapons raised, both crossbows and guns. I follow her gaze and this must be her knight. She's hot in a rugged sort of way. Everything about her exudes power from the clothes she wears to the way she wears her braids.

"Get the fuck away from her, bitch!" her knight shouts.

"Drop the weapon and get on your knees!" a muscular man yells.

"Oh, this is going to be fun," I purr and look up at my shadow. "She can be a canvas or a punishment doll, I'll let you decide. Maybe I'll immortalize this fight on her skin and give her the eternal kiss so you can spend the centuries suffering together."

"You okay, sugar?" her knight asks.

Little Shadow shakes her head. "I know you come…"

Her knight turns to me. "You must be the monster she's so afraid of."

I could take my time and play with them, instead I'm going to show them why she's so afraid of me.

They unload their clips and bows as fast as their pathetic little fingers can go. The impressive manpower dwindles, reinforcements come and die, it all comes down to the knight and what I want to do with her.

Little Shadow sobs, hope blown out of her with all the blood and bullets. "Don't hurt her," she begs.

"On the contrary, she's going to tell me just how much she enjoys what I'm going to do."

The fear is palpable, but the Hunter tries to mask it. "Fuck you, I'm not gonna end up like them."

"No, you'll end up like her," I gesture to Little Shadow. "I'll paint this night on you, then give you an eternal kiss."

The Hunter attacks, Hawthorne wood stakes coming up from cuffs in her sleeves. We fight, I'm a cat playing with a mouse, she's out for blood. I get her, and take a taste, she's magnificent.

"Mmm, I get it now," I say to my shadow. "She tastes heavenly."

Little Shadow is fighting to get off the wall, I'm distracted by her, and the Hawthorne drives into my chest. It would have been a kill shot, but I'm a mirror of others, organs on the opposite side as they're supposed to be.

"Fuck you, bitch!" she says using the force she stabbed me with knocking me back to the floor.

In the time she takes to realize something is amiss, I have her shackled to a place at the feet of my shadow.

"That was fun." I look at my canvas. "You're going to get a break," then I turn to the Hunter who is fighting viciously. "It's your turn."

⊹⊱⊰⊹

The canvas is long dead. As is my little doe, I'd hunt her down, and she'd escape, Little Shadow or her Knight helping her instead of themselves countless times. Every time I'd get her back, it didn't matter where she ran. Sometimes I'd let her settle, believe she was safe. She met a sweet woman; they got married, had kids. Oh, the beautiful and unspeakable things I did to her wife, her kids, her grandkids. Now I wander the radiation-soaked ruins the humans and their wars left behind looking for a new toy to stave off the boredom.

Pardon, Refuted
Rachel Dill

There were some who called Pierce 'King'. Pierce scoffed at it, sneering at the idea she might be counted amongst the fat pigs who lounged in their thrones amongst their furs and sent others out to do their killing. She never stopped them though; they said it with reverence, with fear and pride mixing together until Pierce was as powerful to them as the ocean. Pierce's hatred of kings did not outweigh her affection for power.

Ysa, Pierce's quartermaster, suspected she was the only one who understood how insulting of a title 'King' was to her captain. A king sat and whined and sent out dogs, and protested and quivered at the idea he may have to do any true work of his own. A king did not sport calluses on his hands and feet from running up and down the decks during storms, pulling tight on the lines to keep the sails in check, gripping the wheel with bloody hands to keep the ship from being smashed to pieces on the rocks. Kings did not growl back when sea monsters reared their hideous heads from the waves, did not man the guns when fresh recruits were paralyzed with terror. The only title worthy of Pierce was 'Captain'.

Ysa could begrudge that there were enough 'captains' in the little pirate nest of Uassan to make it unreasonable to give the same title to their unofficial leader. Still. 'King' was a poor fit.

Pierce was looking out the tall windows of her cabin. The crew might jump at the chance to sleep in real beds without the sea rocking underneath them, but Pierce and Ysa rarely left the ship save on business. They were creatures of the sea in a way most pirates could only pretend to be. They had not gone to sea just to cling to the land whenever it drifted close.

"Government ship just slunk into dock," Pierce said, her gravelly voice cool and even. She might have been idly commenting on the clouds drifting past overhead. But Ysa knew her well, knew she was like the ocean - stillness could mean death just as surely as any storm.

"Which government?"

"Rouvalon." Her voice stayed even, but as Ysa stepped up to see for herself, she caught the curl of disgust on Pierce's lip.

"Cocky bastards. What do you suppose they want?"

"Our unconditional surrender, no doubt. Perhaps for us to tie up our own nooses and trot happily off to dance a jig in Central Square."

Ysa didn't know anything of Pierce's past. The woman may as well have been spat out of the ocean, fully formed, as have a human mother who'd once tucked her in at night. But her accent was a coarse Rouvalon one, and Ysa followed her captain too closely to have missed that they were Pierce's favorite ships to sink.

"He must believe his God can find him out here," Ysa said, watching as a young man in a crisp uniform stepped off his ship and onto the pier, shadowed by a small cluster of soldiers. "Will we be showing him he's wrong?"

Pierce didn't answer, only watched their newcomer quietly, slowly tilting her head to keep her good eye locked on him. The other eye, shiny white and surrounded by twisted burns, was a topic of much gossip amongst the rabble. Ysa had never asked about it. Nothing before Pierce had become her captain was her business.

They watched the man stride down the pier, head held high. If he conceived of how willing and able the people surrounding him were of splitting him in half, he showed no fear of it. Ysa attributed that more to arrogance than courage. Likely nobility, in a clean, untorn uniform like that. They could never wrap their minds around their own mortality, not until they were choking on a sword.

For their parts, the pirates of Uassan were watching him like animals who thought their next meal might be stolen. Uassan was a place of peace, a place for a breather and a good meal between weeks on the ocean, soaking their decks in blood. There were no true laws here, but implicit ones had flowered, particularly in the stability that had flourished in the year and change since Pierce had put the last King's - one more deserving of the title - head on a spear at the end of the docks. One of the strongest rules was that Uassan was no place for a big fight, not when there were so many more profitable ones to be had on the ocean. But this newcomer wouldn't know that, wouldn't *respect* that. So, the pirates watched him with bated breath and waited for him to make the first move.

"Go listen to what he wants," Pierce ordered, stepping back from her window and picking up her sword belt. "I'll be along in a minute."

Ysa nodded and slipped out of the captain's quarters. Pierce had something planned - she always did. On some ships the quartermaster was the only crewman worth a damn - the one who made sure the gunpowder was dry and the sails were patched, that the crew wasn't on the brink of mutiny, that there was enough food and water in the hold to last them until they reached safe harbor again. Not so aboard the *Whale Fall*. Ysa was vital, she knew, watching for all the little details that could sink a ship, but Pierce was far more than the flashy fighter who led the men into battle that some captains were. Pierce was a schemer. An ambitious planner. A woman who would let you run on ahead just to be in a better position to pounce when you thought you'd escaped.

Ysa had spent a very long time looking over her shoulder. She enjoyed knowing someone meaner was now looking over hers.

Their visitor had placed himself in the center of town - or the closest thing Uassan had to one, anyway - and was unfurling a piece of parchment, tied with a ribbon, with the crest of Rouvalon's king pressed into it. He was definitely a noble - he was speaking in a loud, clear voice with a perfectly dignified accent that sounded like he needed to practice it every morning. "-And so, any pirate who turns himself in by the turn of the new year will be granted a full pardon for his crimes and given a small amount of silver to begin his new life as an honest citizen. So speaks his Imperial Highness, King Archibald Rouvalon the Second."

The man rolled his parchment back up again and looked around expectantly. Pirates watched him warily, waiting for the trap, the catch. A whisper flitted through the crowd like a fly and then multiplied until the buzz could not be ignored. Ysa caught only bits of them, hushed and overlapping as they were, but she understood the intent. Pirates of lower education or foreign languages checking with their crewmates if they had heard the visitor right - if pirates were to be welcomed back to Rouvalon with open arms and no mention of their crimes.

All Ysa heard were squeaks of desperation. The piracy problem had ceased to be a nuisance - now it was a threat. A threat Rouvalon - or any other country - had been unable to get its teeth into for years. Now they were handing the pliers over to the pirates, in the hopes they would remove their own teeth and return home as docile lambs instead of wild wolves.

Ysa had never set foot in Rouvalon. She doubted the pardon was meant for her. Even if it were, she'd have sooner cut off her own head than play meek and humble for men who'd never cracked a blister.

Pierce appeared at her side like a mist. One moment not there at all, the next impossible to ignore. When Ysa looked up her captain's expression was as unreadable as ever, but her outfit said everything. On board the *Whale Fall*, Pierce might dress as captain or crewmate - might wear fine boots or might go barefoot as most of the crew did, for extra purchase on the deck. Might wear her long coat or might choose rough shirts that could be easily sacrificed to the wind and the spray of salt. Typically went bareheaded, lest the wind blow her hat away.

On the shores of Uassan, she was different. She might be a crewmate to the *Whale Fall*'s workers, but she was no comrade to the average citizen of Uassan. She went amongst them not unlike the King they referred to her as - a long red coat of well refined leather, unscuffed boots with buckles that shone, a fine tricorn hat with its long feather of some beautiful bird, pistols with ivory handles hanging from a belt laced with tiny pearls. The eye she was blind in was now covered by an eyepatch with a golden jolly roger stitched into the fabric. It hid the eye, but it somehow left you wondering if something far worse than a blinded eye was tucked away beneath it. The scars still showed, twisting away under the black patch like they had somewhere important to be.

Pierce was no king because no king could ever have hoped to escape her shadow, had they found themselves in a room with her.

"I was wondering when they'd start trying to coax us all back home," Pierce said demurely. Ysa wondered if this was a trick that had been tried before. She had never learned much history - of Rouvalon or anywhere else - but Pierce often spent hot, windless days reading in her cabin. She may have come across any number of tactics for governments trying to haul their wayward citizens back into line.

Ysa looked over the crowd. Some were beginning to look interested in this offer. Others looked wary, still expecting it might only be a ploy to lower their guard. The members of the *Whale Fall*, mostly women, mostly escapees from lovely kingdoms like Rouvalon, looked as disdainful as Ysa felt. A few had noticed Pierce's arrival and had their eyes locked on her and their teeth showing, eager to see how their captain would respond.

Pierce did not keep them waiting. She stepped forward, taking off her hat in a mockery of politeness. "You're from Rouvalon yourself, then?" she asked their visitor.

The man inclined his head politely. Ysa wondered how it twisted at his pride, faking such honors towards pirates. She imagined he could scarcely stomach it. "Indeed, I am my good s-" He stumbled on the words.

Several crewmembers from the *Whale Fall* grinned: sharp, vicious things. Ysa felt her own mouth doing the same. The man had realized he was talking to a woman, and from there it was only a hair's breadth to realizing he was face-to-face with the pirate whose bounty now included a promise of lordship.

Pierce's mouth pulled up like a lazy smile. Ysa had seen a similar one many times on the faces of cats who were playing with mice. The kill wasn't necessary, but it would be enjoyed all the same.

"-My good lady," the man managed at last, trying to recover himself. "You must be the infamous Captain Pierce."

"I'm flattered to be recognized. You must be the spineless dog hoping to root out some vermin in exchange for a pat on the head."

A wave of snickering washed through the crowd. Those who had looked to be considering the pardon were looking towards Pierce now, reminded of where the true law lay, and remembering just how useless fancy lords like this always were in the end.

Their visitor frowned but, to his credit, didn't throw down a gauntlet in defense of his honor. They'd probably specifically chosen someone with the good sense to not enter into duels with pirates. Anyone with half a brain knew they'd cheat.

Pierce pushed back her coat and ran her work-worn fingers along the handles of her guns. "What *do* they know about me in the *civilized world* these days? Last I heard there was a rumor I was the spawn of the sea herself, out to drown every legitimate businessman trying to earn a silver off her back."

"There are always rumors," the man said. "But rest assured, captain, however ruthless your reputation, this pardon does apply to you. Hang up your sword, return to Rouvalon, and you will be granted a full pardon and the opportunity to start anew."

"A tempting offer," Pierce agreed. The crowd, which had fallen silent as soon as Pierce had stepped forward, somehow grew even more quiet. Some of them had survived the experience of seeing Pierce be polite and gracious before, and they knew where this was destined to end. Others hadn't, but they knew a shark waiting to dart forward when they saw one. "Do you know why I became a pirate, little dog?"

There was a pause. Ysa guessed the man was trying to determine if he was expected to answer.

"I imagine," he said, once it was clear the question wasn't rhetorical, "that you felt yourself trapped in an untenable situation. That you wished to better your position and felt you lacked other options."

Pierce tilted her head, so that it seemed it was the jolly roger on the eyepatch that met the man's eyes, not her own. Ysa imagined he felt hunted, caught in the crosshairs of the grinning skull.

"I love how you all always say *felt*," Pierce said. "As though we were only imagining it. As though just around the corner were men giving out bread for free and offering medicine in exchange for trash scrounged off the streets." Pierce looked around at her captive audience who watched with bated breath.

"I didn't turn to piracy for the wealth," Pierce said, and it was unclear, even to Ysa, who exactly the captain was speaking to now. "Though I certainly enjoy that part. I didn't come for the violence. I could have found that slaughtering enemy soldiers on the king's front lines. As much as I love her, I didn't even come for the sea. I could have had her as a navy man. No, I think this is a good time for all assembled to know that I became a pirate because I really, *really-*"

Ysa had spent the better part of two years at Pierce's side, moving in time with her during battles and storms, standing in Pierce's blind spot to cover her, making sure Pierce remembered to eat when her schemes seized her mind, and she didn't leave her cabin for days. And it was only this experience that allowed Ysa to see the flash of movement that was Pierce drawing a gun - not the fancy ivory ones, something more sturdy and reliable - and blasting a shot through the young noble's head.

"-*Really* hate the rich folks of Rouvalon," Pierce finished as the man's body hit the ground like an overfilled sack.

There was a moment of shocked silence. One of the pirates barked a laugh, shattering it, and the young man's guards attacked.

Ysa's hand fell to her sword, but she didn't move. Pierce would tell her if she needed backup. Until then, Ysa would only be in the way.

Pierce's sword flashed and cut one guard through the gut before he was in arm's reach of her. Another's sword swung down for her head, but her own sword was up, catching it, and then she was kicking his knee back until it relented and swung the wrong way with a *snap* like the sound of a ruined mast. She lost interest in the guard the moment his wailing began, spinning to face the last two.

They'd managed a flicker of thought, instead of the too-fast charge their comrades had tried. Their strategy wasn't bad, but they were arrogant idiots if they thought it was one Pierce wouldn't have seen before. One feinted at her right. The other dove in at her left, hiding himself in her blind spot.

As though no one had ever done *that* before. As though no one saw the eyepatch and assumed it must be her week point. As though a woman like Pierce wouldn't have dedicated herself to outwitting such a maneuver.

Pierce went for the man in her blind spot first, slamming a dagger into the back of his neck as he ducked low to aim a shot at her ribs. That put her two steps farther back than the one remaining guard had expected, which gave her plenty of time to grab a fresh pistol and fire a bullet into his heart.

Someone in the crowd started up a cheer and Pierce rewarded their enthusiasm with a quick flash of a grin.

"You'll never get-" the guard still breathing managed, his voice high and panicked with pain and terror, clutching at his unnaturally bent leg.

Ysa assumed he was trying to tell her she wouldn't get away with this. He didn't get a chance to prove her right, because they were all knocked deaf by the boom of cannons, the splintering of wood, and the explosion of gunpowder as the ship the Rouvalons had sailed in on was blasted to pieces.

The guard still breathing went as white as his dead comrades. The pirates clasped hands over their ears, but they grinned at nudged at each other with their elbows. *That's our King,* they all said silently.

Once the ringing in everyone's ears had faded away, Pierce looked over at Ysa. "Make a note I've promised Kyrell my share of our next catch."

Ysa nodded. She was impressed, a rare feeling for her. Kyrell's dramatic timing had been perfect. The gunshot must have been the cue, but that made it no less noteworthy that the gunner had destroyed the ship in such a clean, swift stroke.

Pierce stepped up to the sole survivor of the Rouvalon crew. "You're in luck, my friend," she told him, lightly resting the toe of her boot on his ruined knee. "Some friends of mine will be making sure you return to Rouvalon safe and sound, to deliver His Majesty our response to his generous offer."

Uassan filled with laughter, with cries of *"That's our Pirate King!"* and *"Knew the captain wouldn't stand for the likes of him stinking up our port!"*

But Uassan was a free port filled with free pirates, and that meant there was no such thing as a perfect consensus.

"And so, the tyrant lifts her head at last," someone sneered, stepping free of the crowd. So many had gathered that it was as though he'd walked into an arena with the press of bodies for walls. "Great talk about any man being allowed to do what they like, until there's a risk of them doing something she doesn't agree with."

Ysa looked the challenger over. Captain Vinson. Decent captain, whose crew didn't complain too much. Brought in a decent share of goods on a decent enough basis. Loved attention though, and would sooner kill a bar full of witnesses than allow word to get out that he'd shown weakness. Ysa hadn't seen him before the excitement had begun, but she was willing to bet he'd been considering taking the offer, and now he had to make it seem like the braver thing to do.

Ysa tried to remember who was on his crew. Who would likely end up captaining the *Vixen* once her captain was sent down to the locker? Someone more agreeable? Or someone she and Pierce would need to put the fear of the ocean into?

Pierce appraised Vinson, then stepped over to the dead noble. The man's eyes were still open. He hadn't even had time for shock to overtake his features. Pierce bent down and retrieved the parchment he'd read off, then tossed it to Vinson. "If you'd like to accompany our friend here," she nudged at the guard, who whimpered in response, "back to Rouvalon and take your pittance of silver, be my guest. I have no interest in having to look at a coward's face every time I go into the market."

"Of course. You killed him because you're so willing to let all your loyal subjects go."

"Were you not listening, Captain? I killed him because I hate Rouvalon's wealthy. And most of their poor, if I'm being honest. It was purely personal." She turned her back on Vinson and spun slowly, facing the crowd circling her a bit at a time. "Anyone who wants to return home and put this colorful patch of life behind them is welcome to, as far as I'm concerned. Here, it is every man and woman for themselves, every moral code to be individually decided. I won't stand in your way."

She turned back to Vinson. "But once you decide, leave fast. Because if you take that offer, you're no longer a pirate. You'll be an honest citizen of Rouvalon." She pushed against the head of one of the dead guards with her foot, twisting it so his lifeless eyes looked up at Vinson. "And I *hate* honest citizens of Rouvalon. And for the sakes of all the serpents in the seas, don't involve *me* in your decision. I also hate people who don't have enough of a spine to make their own choices. *That's* why I turned to piracy. I hoped to have to look at fewer yellow-livered cowards when I woke up every morning. One more whine about it out of you - out of any of you!-" she shouted the last bit- "And

I'll give you the same bullet between the eyes our spineless friend received."

She turned towards Ysa. Ysa grinned, as pleased as always to watch her captain turn her opposition into so much wasted air, and then her expression froze as Vinson lunged to catch Pierce from behind.

Maybe Pierce saw the warning that flashed through Ysa's eyes. Maybe the stories that she'd traded that blinded eye for a better kind of vision were true. Maybe Vinson breathed through his mouth too loudly and a drunk could have heard him coming.

Whichever it was, Pierce leaped nimbly to one side and Vinson missed, his blade catching and tearing along the folds of her coat.

"You know what?" Pierce said. "I lied about the bullet." Steel flashed in the hot sun. She pounced, knocking Vinson to the ground, his own blade skittering away from him, and she plunged a dagger into his forehead, his skull crunching beneath the blade like the shell of a lobster.

"Mewling louts like you aren't worth the ammunition," she told Vinson's freshly lifeless body.

She wrenched the dagger free, stood, and began to move for the dock where the *Whale Fall* waited. "Make your own decisions," she ordered the assembled pirates. "I'm not your fucking mother."

A Gut Feeling
Kay Hanifen

Today had been a good day. Alidred the Malevolent had woken up, ate some of her trigger foods, and worked out without any of her usual…embarrassing issues. It was supposed to be her day, the day all her plans came to fruition, and she couldn't afford to spend most of it on the toilet.

Donning her armor, she sat sideways on her throne, one leg thrown up around the arm, waiting to hear back from her troops.

Her top general, Rivener, slammed open the massive doors. "Lord Alidred."

She waved him forward. "What?"

"We've got her, sir."

She sat up, her attention piqued. "You found the latest one chosen to defeat me?"

He grinned, revealing his sharp, pointed teeth. "More like she found us. The foolish girl thought she could sneak into the place and take you out while we weren't paying attention."

"So, she's dead?"

When her general fell silent and glanced away, she arched an eyebrow. Rivener awkwardly cleared his throat. "Not quite. She had something on her that we thought you'd want to see."

She leaned forward, resting her elbows on her knees. "Well, don't just stand there. Bring her in."

He opened the door and two of his foot soldiers appeared, dragging a girl between them. They stopped in front of the dais and forced the woman to her knees. She looked surprisingly young. Alidred was not adept at telling human ages from simple appearances, but the girl looked to be in her early twenties. Her hair had been cut close to her head, giving her a boyish appearance. Alidred tried not to think about how this girl was exactly her type. She wasn't above beatings and torture, but there were lines even she wouldn't cross.

The armor that the chosen one wore was lightweight and ill-fitting as though she'd borrowed it from someone else. The girl was obviously unprepared, but that was no surprise. Every once and a while, she'd get a "chosen one" thrown at her. Almost all of them were everymen with almost no combat experience. They were called chosen ones because they were literally appointed to kill her by cowards who would rather believe in prophecies and saviors than fight her on the field of battle. This was nothing new to her.

Instead, the thing that caught Alidred's eye was the sword. The legendary Blade of Magnamar was truly a sight to behold. The steel seemed to glow as though it was still burning in the forge, but she knew it would be cold to the touch if she handled it. The weapon was centuries old but had no nicks, flecks of rust or burns from when she'd hid it in a volcano. It was purported to be the only weapon forged that could kill her, which was why she had been so careful about making sure that no one but her could access it. Where did this lowly girl in her ill-fitting armor find it?

Alidred sauntered down the steps and lifted the girl's face by the chin to get a better look at her. The woman's defiant eyes were so brown they were almost black. She snarled.

Only for the threat to be undercut by the grumbling of the girl's stomach. A look of panic crossed her face before she hid it with a glare.

Alidred smiled. "Are you hungry, little chosen one?"

"No," she replied forcefully, only for her stomach to grumble again. She hunched in on herself, looking pale and clammy. Alidred recognized that look, that pain like hot nails being screwed into the lower gut. The girl sighed. "This is really embarrassing, but before you start torturing me, can I run to the restroom?"

Rivener laughed. "Plenty of people's bowels have been evacuated in the face of Alidred the Malevolent. You should consider yourself lucky to be in her presence."

"It's not because I'm scared," the girl gritted out.

"So, you're trying to deceive our mistress and escape?"

Alidred suppressed an eyeroll. Her right-hand man meant well but could be over the top. She waved a hand and the door to her private toilet chambers opened. "Go. Make it quick." She told herself that she only did this because the alternative was having the girl shit herself, which would have been unpleasant for everyone involved.

The girl did a double take. "Wait, really?"

"But my lord, this could be a ruse so she could escape," Rivener protested.

This time, she did roll her eyes. "Divest her of her weapons and armor. Quickly. And then I'll be with her in there."

They did as she ordered—the removal of the sword loosening an anxious knot in her chest—and once it was done, the girl ran off to the bathroom with Alidred close behind. She shut the door and locked the two of them in before turning on the fan and facing the wall.

"Why are you doing this?" the girl said once the worst of the emergency was over. Alidred knew that she'd want to stay there a few minutes more in case of aftershocks. It's what she did, after all.

"I don't mind blood but shit smells bad. Don't care for it." As though it wanted to personally betray her, her stomach grumbled. And it had been such a good day until this point.

"Oh, you have it too!" the girl exclaimed. "So annoying, right?"

"And embarrassing. I will do everything in my power to ensure that it never gets out. Memory spells are tricky and dangerous, but I'm not above using it."

The girl laughed. "Trust me. It won't leave this bathroom."

Alidred sighed at the demands of her guts. "And at this rate, neither will we. What's your name?"

"Yura," she said. "I'm supposed to kill you, but now it feels awkward."

Alidred smirked. "Yes, I would prefer not to die on the toilet if I can help it."

"And I would prefer not to be tortured, if that's at all possible."

She shrugged. "We'll see."

After both had done their business, they retired to Lord Alidred's private chambers, much to the confusion of Rivener. Yura sat on her couch while Alidred poured them both glasses of wine. A servant appeared with some breads, meats, and cheeses to enjoy with it.

"So, I have to ask," Yura said. "Why are you doing this? You seem pretty reasonable. Why are you trying to take over the world?"

Alidred set the glasses on the table in front of them. "When I was a child, I watched my family be murdered right in front of me by the king's soldiers. I was helpless then but swore to myself that I would never be weak like that again." A story like that was bound to elicit sympathy, regardless of whether or not it was true.

"I'm sorry." Yura held the drink in her hands without taking a sip. *Smart girl.*

Alidred smirked. "It's very good wine, you know."

"Alcohol rarely agrees with me."

"I'm sure that this will. Here. We'll trade." She took a sip from her glass and then handed it to Yura before taking the other girl's glass. She took a sip of Yura's glass as well. "See? Not poisoned."

Yura smiled, her cheeks coloring rather adorably as she took a sip of her own. "It is quite good. Thank you."

She hadn't poisoned it. Not yet anyway. She wanted to give Yura a chance. After all, as much as he objected to snacks and wine with the enemy, Rivener had been telling her that she should get out more. She leaned in closer, flipping her raven hair over her shoulder. "And what about you? How did you get your hands on the Blade of Magnamar?"

Yura shrugged. "Found it."

"You just found it?" Alidred arched an incredulous eyebrow. "I hid it someplace where no mere mortal could safely tread."

"Inside Mount Hellgate." Yura smirked, and Alidred felt all the blood rush to her head, dizzying her. "How much do you know about volcanoes?"

She shrugged. "It's appropriately inhospitable to most forms of life."

Yura grinned and leaned even closer. "It's also a shield volcano. You wouldn't know this because you're not from the area, but a shield volcano has frequent minor eruptions. Think of it like a runny nose when other, quieter volcanoes are like a sneeze. Are you following so far?" As she spoke, she gesticulated animatedly, apparently eager to share this with anyone who would listen…including the woman holding her captive. It was oddly endearing to watch the way her eyes lit up when Yura talked about the types of volcanoes.

Amused, Alidred nodded. *Where was she going with this?* "Are you from the area, then?"

She shook her head. "Oh, no. I just study volcanoes. I was in the area taking samples of the pyroclastic flow when I saw the sword just floating by. Naturally, I had to know how that was possible, so I picked it up, and all the locals got super excited. They threw this armor on me and sent me here to kill you."

Alidred sat back in her seat, surprised. The locals had made it abundantly clear that they wanted her gone, but Yura was comically underqualified for the job, even by chosen one standards. "Well, do you want to kill me?"

"I guess that depends."

Alidred arched her eyebrows. "On what?"

"Your plan, mostly. What do you actually want to do with the kingdom once you have it."

"Kill the king and all his sycophants."

"And then what?" Yura asked mildly as she took another sip of her wine.

Alidred blinked her thoughts slowing. Did she drink on an empty stomach again? "What do you mean?"

Staring impassively at her captor, Yura took another sip of her wine. "Well, you got rid of the old guys—great job—but a revolution only lasts when you have a plan put into place. Most dictatorships fail after a few years because the guy in charge is so obsessed with power and control that he starts restricting his people way too much, leading to a revolution. And the cycle continues." She tilted her head. "So, what makes you different from the last guy or the one who comes after you? Do you have a tax policy written out? What about plans for the country's imports and exports? How will you make sure that the people stay on your side? Fear will only rule them for so long. Eventually, they'll get fed up and demand change or you'll be ousted."

Suddenly, this conversation had stopped being fun. Alidred poured the last of her glass of wine down her throat without tasting it. "I should have you beaten for your impertinence."

"Maybe." Yura finished her wine. "But you know I'm right. Conquerors rarely make great rulers, especially if they measurably change the lives of the small folk for the worse."

"Tell me, oh wise volcano scientist, what I should do instead," Alidred replied through gritted teeth. This girl had some nerve to come in and criticize her for the way she ruled. With a crack, the glass shattered in her hand, leaving shards embedded in shredded skin.

Yura shrugged and took Alidred's hand. The Lord of Malevolence did her best not to blush. "Take up knitting?" Yura suggested. "Learn to garden? I understand that you want revenge for the death of your family, but conquest will only hurt those that you never meant to hurt."

This was ridiculous. Why should she care about the words of a lowly scientist in borrowed armor? Sure, Yura was cute, but if she's going to insist on this self-righteous moralizing, things were about to get really boring really fast. "It would be in your best interest to mind your tongue," Alidred growled.

Yura wore a bland smile on her face and reached over to spread some strawberry jam on bread. "Perhaps. But I'm afraid someone has to say it."

"No, you're not afraid. But you will be. Rivener?"

"Yes, my lord?" came the voice of her right-hand man as he poked his head through the door.

"I've grown bored of the prisoner. Take her to the dungeon." She got to her feet, only to sway unsteadily. Why did she suddenly feel woozy?

Yura kept that bland smile on her face. "Don't worry. It's just a sleeping draught. Think about what I said, because I like you. You're gorgeous. It would be a shame for you to continue the cycle of tyrants." *That little bitch.*

She fell to her knees, watching helplessly as Yura attacked Rivener with far more skill than what she would expect from a scientist. She knocked him out, and Alidred closed her eyes, bracing for the end. She felt a hand on hers and heard the sound of footsteps fade down the hall. And then, world faded to nothing.

She woke with a massive hangover and a note shoved up her sleeve.

Alidred,

I had a good time with you. Hopefully, we won't have to try to kill each other again any time soon, because I really do like you.

XOXO,
Yura

In spite of herself, Alidred grinned and held the note close to her chest. She underestimated Yura.

The girl may have won this round, but Alidred couldn't wait to match wits with her again.

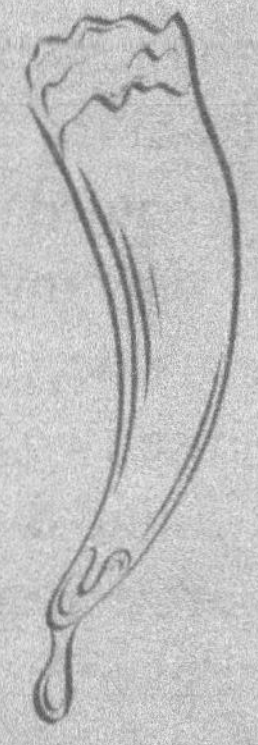

Metu Sanguinis
Sarah Rossino

I sat on the floor at the far end of the dancefloor. Not a single part about this week made any sense to me at all. I was broken up with, nearly hit by a car crossing the street, and just a few days ago, some stranger held me against a wall and bit me in the neck. I'm not even sure why I didn't fight them back either. Was it because they were kind of cute and the needed affection from losing my partner earlier in the week was in overdrive? Perhaps. But whatever the reason, they left some nasty scar on my neck that I've tried covering up with everything. It was becoming harder to hide than the kiss marks on my neck I would have to keep from my mom and dad when I came home late on a Saturday night.

I didn't even know why my legs brought me to this low-lit club. I hadn't been dancing since Jared started seeing other guys two months ago. Funny how he never knew I found out, but I just thought it was a phase he'd grow out of at some point. Jokes on me I guess, right? Now I'm just here in a thrown together shirt and tie sitting on the floor of a club like a teenager that just got rejected to slow dance with his crush at the school dance. I'm surprised security hasn't tried scooping me up and throwing me to the curb, but what's even stranger is everyone that walks by me seems to startle a bit. To be fair, I would be too if I saw some grown man sitting on the floor of a club looking miserable.

But those people aren't the only ones that have startled while walking past me in the last few days. Ever since that psycho on the street bit my neck, it's been a weird time around anyone that gets too close. Maybe they sense I let weirdos bite me on the street and don't want to be the next one in my shoes. Whatever the reason, I've taken heavy notice to it. I will admit though, ever since that guy bit me, I've been feeling really strange. The sunlight hurts my entire body, I'm more active when the sun goes down, and worst of all, I have this burning in my throat that just won't go away.

Look, I've always been one that's been sensitive to the sun. Thanks genetics. But now it's like the moment I step out into the light, my entire body starts to fry like I'm in some kind of air fryer with the setting on high. Even with long sleeves and pants, I'm still cooking. It's kept me inside during the day which is fine because I don't work in the mornings anymore. Jared ruined that for me by blackmailing me over at the post office. I knew they always liked him more than me anyway. But the night thing? That's not like me at all. I've always been one to be dead tired by around nine o'clock, but lately it's when I start becoming more awake. I've been laying up all through the night now only feeling tired when the sun starts to rise. I guess it's just another good reason I don't work the mornings anymore.

Now the burning in my throat is something I really am starting to think I should get checked out. I'm not one for going to the doctor but it's been so bad, anything I try and eat just won't go down. I've thrown up at least four times in the last few days whenever I tried eating something and it just seems off. The last time I had a meal was Thursday night, right before that strange man got all up close and personal. I mean, I always wanted to go on a diet, but not like this. I guess I'll just have to muster up some courage and call the doctor in the morning if I'm not asleep then.

"Ow!"

The sudden sound of someone's voice snapped me back to reality as I saw a girl laying on the floor with shattered glass at her feet. I gasped at the sight as I could see she must've gotten hurt, her friends not paying much mind to her as I could hear them just laughing from the bar. I quickly got to my feet and ran over to her; her makeup was running down her face as I could see she was crying.

"Oh honey! Are you okay?!" I extended my hand to her which she took rather quickly.

She didn't say anything as she slowly got to her feet, glass falling off of her dress and onto the floor with a clatter. In my panic to help her, I hadn't even noticed she was clutching her arm. It didn't hit me what had happened until I could suddenly smell the blood. It caught me so off guard, I staggered back from her. I was never one for blood but the fact that I could smell it frightened me more than the sight of it.

"I-I'm okay," she stammered, trying to reach out the hand that was now covered in blood to me.

What was worse to me was that as my eyes drifted to the blood that was trickling down her fingers, the burn in my throat only seemed to get worse. I clutched my throat with my hand, not thinking much of it as I tried to just get away from her. I ran through the crowd of dancers, bumping into many of them until I was out the door and back on the sidewalk. There was no more loud music or dozens of people talking at once, just the sounds of cars speeding by the club and the wind winding itself through the buildings.

"Hey kid, you alright?"

I didn't even know where the voice was coming from at first as I let go of my throat, the burning a little more manageable. I tried taking a long, deep breath but that only seemed to make the burn intensify.

"Kid?"

I turned around to find the bouncer looking at me funny. I tried to force a smile, but all I could do was cry. The look of concern on his face softened as he came closer to me, extending an arm around my shoulder before giving me a harsh pat on the back, "You get broken up with, kid? It's alright. It happens to all of us. Why don't you just head home and get some sleep. You look terrible."

I didn't understand why his closeness to me made the burn worsen but I didn't want to be rude to his comfort. I needed an embrace after these last few days so I stuck it out the best I could before pulling away from him and walking towards home.

Normally I would've gotten an Uber but the thirty-minute walk to my apartment just seemed well needed. I should've thanked that bouncer for being so polite, but it was too late now. I just needed to get home and figure out what was going on with me. Maybe I'll just call the doctor and leave them a voicemail to get to in the morning. Any kind of help now would be much appreciated.

I walked down the street with my hands buried in my pockets. The wind blew back my tie over my shoulder that I gave up trying to fix. There were so many things I wanted answers to that I just knew wouldn't be easy to figure out in a night. Why did the sun burn me alive now? Why was I so awake during the night now? Why is food so appalling to me now? And why did that girl's blood smell so…good?

"Damn. You look worse than when I found you."

I didn't even startle at the unsuspecting voice this time. I was so focused on going home, I didn't even stop to engage where the voice had come from.

"What, so I give you a new sense of purpose and you just walk away from me without even a thank you?"

I stopped in my tracks. What did they just say? A new sense of purpose?

"Ah, so that got your attention. I don't think we ever got properly introduced," I heard footsteps suddenly come from the alleyway as I turned around to find a man that looked all too familiar. "You passed out before I was even finished, I never got the chance. The name's Byron."

"O-Okay? S-So what do you want?" I didn't even try to hide the nervousness in my tone as I spoke.

"So that's it?" Byron chuckled. "I don't get to know who you are?"

"I-I'm Fletcher, but everyone just calls me Fletch."

"Fletch, huh? I like that," he smirked, immediately making me flush a little. "Listen Fletch, I feel you're in need of an apology. I didn't exactly stick around long enough to fill you in on everything before ditching you the other night. I just had to be somewhere else, and I figured I'd find you eventually and I'm glad I was right. So, I guess I'll start with I'm sorry."

"What...what are you talking about? You know, ever since you attacked me the other night, nothing has been right. Everything has been a living nightmare and I need answers," I hated how demanding I was sounding but after the night I was having, I sort of didn't care.

Byron chuckled again, taking a few steps forward into the light of the streetlamp revealing his vibrant blonde hair and blue eyes, "Demanding. I like that."

I immediately flushed more, hoping he wouldn't see but the amused look in his eyes told me he could see everything.

"You deserve some answers, Fletch, and that's why I'm glad I found you wandering around out here. For the record though, I didn't just attack you. I felt you were a qualifying candidate for my coven so, I jumped on the opportunity. Maybe a little too literally."

"C-Coven?! It's that a group of…"

"Vampires, yes," he interrupted. "But before you lose your head, just listen to me please."

Vampire?! But those things didn't exist! They were just some sparkly men the teenagers always obsessed over in middle school! They were never something that actually existed in the real world!

"Look, I can see your panicking. And before you say something dumb, no, we don't sparkle like those media vampires. That was some falsehood created to mock us or something. Maybe make us look pretty, I don't know the reason, but that's not what we are. We're more than just blood-thirsty killers. We have wars to battle, lives to save. It's why I picked you to join us. You seemed like you needed help."

My fervent questions were put on hold as I looked at him confused, "What do you mean I looked like I needed help? You know nothing about me."

"Jared, right? Your ex?"

Hearing his name again sent needles through my heart. Did he know him?

"I overheard him talking about you at some bar downtown while I was out on my nightly strolls. All he did was talk about how you were so innocent and easy to manipulate which made it easier for him to use you. I didn't want to listen to it, but I just had to. He wouldn't shut up about how much he tricked you into thinking he loved you and it broke me to hear. Stories after stories of all the nice things you did for him, he was talking so horribly about them. I knew I had to save you somehow. You seemed too innocent to let slip away, and I thought if I gave you a new purpose in life, things wouldn't seem so bad."

I was silent for a while. I knew Jared wasn't the greatest partner, but I did love him. Maybe it was stupid of me to do so, but I did. Hearing someone else confirm all the things I was so worried about in the past that was always shot down hurt. It really hurt. I know this guy wasn't trying to dig the needles in further, but they were as far in as they could go. The silence was broken up by a few short sniffles and a weak attempt at hiding the tears into my sleeve.

"Hey, hey, come on now. That's not what I wanted to do, Fletch," Byron took another step closer, now only inches from me as I tried to keep my tears out of sight even though he already saw them. "Listen, that guy doesn't need you. You deserve so much more than some sleezy man who's just out to hurt you. It sounded to me like you were really something and I just wanted to try and help."

"I-I've just had such a terrible week," I lowered my head, letting the tears just fall into my hands as I let myself go.

"Hey now, it's alright," Byron rested his hand on my shoulder. "I'm here to help you I promise. Being in a coven means you have sanctuary, safety, peace. You're safe now from the troubles you had in the past. You can build a new life now; however you so choose. And also," his lips came close to my ears, "you can drain the blood of your enemies."

I immediately stammered back until I lost my footing and hit the sidewalk, "No! I-I can't!"

"What?" Byron chuckled, "Of course you can."

"No! I-I…"

"You're a vampire now you…"

"I'm afraid of blood, okay?!"

There was a heavy silence that fell after my words, the wind even seemed to stop as we just stared at one another. Byron had a concerned look on his face that quickly slipped into a half-smile until suddenly, he burst out laughing. He went on for so long I felt like he wasn't going to stop. I slowly got myself back to my feet, slowly rubbing my arm nervously as I waited for him to stop.

"Wait, wait, wait. So, you're telling me…I turned someone who's afraid of blood…into a vampire?!" his words were broken by his laughter.

"Y-Yeah…" I nervously replied, unsure if he was being serious in his questioning.

Byron slowly stopped his laughter, wiping the tears from his eyes, "I'm sorry, I'm sorry. I just…metu sanguinis."

"Metu what?" I cocked my head at his weird words.

"Metu sanguinis. It's Latin for fear of blood."

"Okay?"

"I was always told at some point there would come a day a vampire would have the condition, but I just couldn't believe it."

"Condition?! Are you saying I'm a sick vampire?!" I crossed my arms at my chest. "You know this isn't exactly going well for a first meeting."

"My apologies. That came out wrong. No, it's not a condition or a sickness. It's something new that vampires have been wanting to try for some time. A sort of, new way to blend amongst the humans without fear of harming them."

"I'm not following."

Byron gestured his head towards the alleyway, "Let's go for a walk."

"A walk? But I want to know what you're talking about!" I demanded.

"You know, Fletch, I think we're going to be great friends," Byron chuckled, annoying me that he wouldn't answer my question.

"Friends?! You're already keeping secrets and you're talking about friends?!"

"Yup. Now come on, we have much to discuss," Byron spoke as he turned around and walked towards the alleyway, not even waiting for me to follow.

I sighed loudly, not wanting to follow him but I figured, what was honestly the worst thing that could happen that hasn't already? I rolled my eyes and ran after the blonde vampire with the pretty blue eyes and started to let my mind ease and wander about what new life was about to unfold for me.

A Murder of Convenience
Tucker Struyk

"Honest people don't hide their deeds."
— Emily Brontë, *Wuthering Heights*

A petite woman of means, clad in an empire waist dress and a stretch-scuba jacket, departed an architectural firm and followed the sidewalk around the block. She held her head high. Her eyeline hovered over passing heads, so as to avoid an intrusive moment of eye contact with a stranger. Foley took full advantage of this by keeping a good ten yards between her and himself. His neon hoodie and ball cap gave him the aura of a tourist on the move. He kept his head on a swivel—making like he was taking in the sights—when, in reality, he was keeping tabs on her. The woman was easy to keep up with in those high heel shoes. Her name was Emery Triggs. She was a big shot architect, an art collector, and kept herself busy with painting, as a hobby—busy enough to arouse suspicion from her spouse. It started out small enough—a meeting here and an exhibit there—until Emery was out late nearly every night of the week. That was where Foley came in. He had been tailing her for days. He maintained his distance but never lost sight of her. During that time, he took notes on where she went and who with. Meantime, she was none-the-wiser. Soon enough, all her comings and goings would be out in the open. Nowhere to run to, nowhere to hide.

Emery came to a halt in front of a fancy Mediterranean restaurant. There, she waited until a woman arrived—a knockout in a pair of platform boots. Emery met the woman with a smile. The two united in a warm embrace. As they parted, their eyes met and ignited a spark of familiarity. They tittered, like two birds of a feather.

Foley removed the high-definition camera he had stashed in the cap of a ballpoint pen and snapped a couple photos of the pair. Emery placed a guiding hand on the small of the woman's back and ushered her into the restaurant. They were seated at a table near the window. Once they were out of view, Foley removed his tourist attire and, beneath, he wore a buttoned-up shirt and slacks. He sauntered by the restaurant window, with his phone held to his ear. "Look, everyone knows, you never catch a falling knife," he said. A phrase common enough for the business district. He paused, as if someone was speaking on the other end. "I'm telling you, don't fight the ticker tape." Meanwhile, he rattled off dozens of photos as he paced in place.

Emery glanced outside. She squinted, under the sun's glare.

Foley shuffled along down the street and took a lap around the restaurant. As he walked, he peeked over his shoulder—to ensure they had not noticed him. His eyes never lingered on them for no longer than an instant. In that time, he clocked them. Emery doted on the woman across from her with a toothy grin and bedroom eyes. Foley sighed. An unabashed smirk took ahold of his lips. He resisted the urge to jump up and down in a victory dance. If only his partner, Wilmot, had been there to witness his first real case and, with it, his first real success—short of a couple tricks on Cora Avenue. His smile faded to a frown. His brows relaxed to a sunken position on his forehead, just above his eyes. In truth, Foley feared Wilmot was embarrassed of him and did not wish for them to be seen together. Wilmot came from an older generation than Foley, a more suppressed one. Despite having lived through Stonewall and the passing of Bill C-150, Wilmot was brought up in a parti pris, insulated locale. A penurious part of town, where a person could be jumped for presenting who they are to the world—at least back in those days. Now, Wilmot's neighborhood was commercial land with an increased median income and a Starbucks on the corner. Still, Foley felt Wilmot was stuck in the past, stuck in the closet.

Foley stationed himself in front of the restaurant. With only one way in and out, Emery was sure to pass him by at some point. In his best Wilmot impression, Foley leaned against the wall and puffed on a vape pen. Just then, Emery walked the woman outside to a ride-share car parked nearby. Foley stood up straight. His eyes did not waver from the car. He flagged down a taxi and told the driver to tail the Toyota Camry. The cab driver groaned from the front seat. "I can't do that," he said. Foley dug a hand into his pocket and pulled out a fifty-dollar bill. Then, just like that, they were off.

A picturesque building, embedded deep in the city's squalid district, once stood as a courthouse; now, it lived on as a hub for wastrels to have untold secrets revealed at a fixed price. Still, the tribunal charm remained. The brick masonry had a symmetry to it, accented by splashes of ashlar stonework. Through the oaken doorway, Foley went over the evidence he had compiled with his client. Wilmot waltzed inside with a bag of bagels and lox from Foley's favorite deli. He plopped down at the desk with them. His eyes and hands were preoccupied with the food in front of him, but his ears were pricked and attentive to the subject at hand. The client faltered, mid-sentence, and stared at Wilmot with her mouth agape. Foley cleared his throat. "I'm sorry, Mrs. Triggs," he said, "how rude of me?" He gestured to the man at his side. "This is my partner, Wilmot."

Wilmot extended a hand to her. "Pleasure to meet you, Mrs. Triggs."

She shook his hand and smiled. Though, her eyes told a different story. "The pleasure is all mine," she said, "and, please, call me Coby."

Foley turned to Wilmot. "I was just going over my findings with Mrs. Triggs," he said. He shot Wilmot daggers. His eyes widened and his head tilted, as a cue for Wilmot to make himself scarce.

Instead, Wilmot set his lunch aside. "Would you mind if I sit in?" he asked. "I promise, I'll be as quiet as a church mouse."

Coby swallowed her annoyance well enough. "Of course," she said, "have a seat." Her silk lashes fluttered to mask an eyeroll. "The more the merrier."

Wilmot scooted his chair closer. His hands folded upon his lap. Foley turned his attention back toward the client. Though, he suddenly felt self-conscious with Wilmot overseeing their conversation. He did his best to ignore the thought. "As I was saying," he said, "I'm afraid your suspicions were correct, Mrs. Triggs." He laid out a mélange of photographs on the desktop. "On the nights of Tuesday and Wednesday, Emery went out to dinner with a young woman. Then, on the night of Thursday, Emery stayed at the woman's apartment until one in the morning. They'd spent the night drinking brandy and lounging in each other's arms, as you can see here."

Coby went over every image with a fine-tooth comb. She gripped the photos so hard they curled at the edges. Her eyes flittered back and forth, as if she were reading a book. She grew desperate— desperate for answers, desperate to unravel some empirical meaning in the twisted games lovers play. "How could she?" she said. "That damn assistant of hers. Blythe is her name. What a harlot she is." Her bottom lip quivered. "Emery told me not to worry when she hired Blythe. Oh, God. What a fool I am."

Wilmot leaned back in his chair. His brow raised to an arch. "I don't understand," he said. "How do these pictures prove infidelity?" He flipped through the evidence himself. "There's no photos of them caught in-the-act, no definite signs of intimacy at all—how do we know they're not in a platonic relationship?"

Coby scoffed. "Excuse me," she said, "I know my wife and I know infidelity when I see it." She snatched the photos from Wilmot's grasp. "Besides, there won't be any kissing or groping to see. Emery is asexual." Her head tilted upward in a pompous manner. "This is about more than sex in the traditional sense of the word."

Wilmot scratched his head. "No offense," he said. Under an attentive façade, Coby bristled at his tone. "If she's asexual, why would she have an affair—or even a wife to begin with?"

Foley nearly leapt out of his seat, but he kept his calm demeanor. His eyes met Wilmot's with an icy gaze. "Asexual doesn't mean aromantic," he said. His hands smacked against the desktop in exegetical gestures. "Sexuality is a spectrum, Wilmot—as you well know."

A chortle escaped Wilmot's lips. He turned to Coby. "I hope you're not thinking of this as bulletproof evidence against your wife," he said, "or you'll be laughed out of divorce court."

Coby clutched her pearls—or, rather, her diamond collar necklace. Her eyes narrowed. "I beg your pardon," she said.

"I'm so sorry, Mrs. Triggs," said Foley. "Please excuse my partner's ignorance." He gave Wilmot a piqued glare but kept his tone buoyant and polite. "In fact, shouldn't you be working on your own case?"

Wilmot nodded along. "Oh," he said, "I believe you're correct." He reached out his hand, once more, for a farewell. "It was lovely to make your acquaintance, Coby. I hope I didn't step on any toes."

She snubbed his handshake with a guffaw and redirected her focus back to Foley. She spoke to Wilmot, but her eyes rested upon Foley, as she said, "None more than to be expected from a plebian."

On his way to the back room, Wilmot stopped. He had half a mind to impart a witty retort but thought better of it. Coby was not the type to take a slight sitting down—neither was he. Under his breath, he chuckled. Then, he shrugged off her ill-humored remark with a toke on his vape pen.

A MURDER OF CONVENIENCE

Nestled in a studio apartment downtown, Blythe lounged on the couch with a glass of wine and a bowl of microwave popcorn. She occasionally glanced up at the screen, when she was not responding to texts. The latest horror film, on some streaming service she could never remember the name of, became her white noise machine. In between jump-scares, there was a knock at her door. She muted the movie. Her eyes darted to the locked door. She approached with indecision. She pressed her eye to the peephole. On the other side of the door, she saw a distorted view of Emery's tousled lob haircut and messy bangs—almost as if she were looking at her lover through a fisheye lens. Emery stood in a state of nerves. Her head turned from side to side, to ensure no one was within earshot. "Open up. I got your message," she said. "We need to talk." Blythe's mien contorted to a parlous comportment. She opened the door and collapsed.

Tenants reported a gunshot and the clip-clopping of high heels across the hall.

The sun ascended a smattering of cumulus clouds and approached the magic hour on another jim-dandy day. Wilmot and Foley toiled away in their office. The private investigators scoured through public records, civil judgements, and set up interviews with people close to the dupes they were hired to expose. The shopkeeper's bell rang. They turned to find Detective Barrett in the doorway. He smirked. Wilmot and Foley rose to their feet to greet him. Detective Barrett saluted them with a warm hello and a crack at Wilmot's age. He laughed hard enough for the three of them. Once the pleasantries were out of the way, he put up a stern face. His eyes lasered in on Foley. "Say," said Detective Barrett, "you don't happen to know a Coby Triggs, do you?"

"Coby? Little out of your league, isn't she?" asked Foley. "What does a blighter like you want with a woman like that?"

"So, you do know her," said Detective Barrett.

Foley balked, until Wilmot stepped in. That gave Detective Barrett pause. Wilmot looked at him cross-eyed. "Hey," he said, "we're not a couple of dolts you can browbeat into submission." He squared up against the homicide detective. "Give it to us straight. Why are you here?"

Detective Barrett threw up his hands. "You caught me," he said, "I'm here on the job, but it's really nothing you two need to concern yourselves with." He gave a wave of dismissal. "I'm just crossing some t's and dotting some i's for an open and shut case."

Foley knitted his brows. "What happened to Coby?" he asked.

"Oh, no," said Detective Barrett, "it's not what you think. It's her wife, Emery. She just confessed to the murder of one Blythe Morello."

Foley staggered back into his desk chair. His eyes glazed over in a thousand-yard stare. He looked bemused. His mind reeled at the thought of what would have driven her to murder and what part he had to play in her mental crack-up. All that time he watched Emery, she never so much as raised her voice. It was hard to imagine what would drive an inhibited woman like her to kill. Not much had changed since then—not for him, anyway. "Why would Emery do that to Blythe?" he asked.

"Blythe used her affair with Emery as blackmail, in order to receive a promotion," said Detective Barrett. "Turns out, Emery didn't take too kindly to that. She came knocking on Blythe's door with a nine-millimeter. When Blythe opened the door expecting a payday, Emery pumped lead into her pretty face." He shuddered. "It was a gruesome scene."

Wilmot and Foley were left dumbfounded. They passed a mournful glance to one another. Their heads hung in remembrance.

Wilmot paced between Foley and the detective. His hand fingered his chin, in thought. He slowed to a standstill, then shot a raised finger to Detective Barrett. "Do you mind if we take a look at the evidence?" he asked.

Detective Barrett shrugged. "Be my guest."

⊰⊹⊱⊰⊹⊱⊰⊹⊱

The city's nearest police precinct took on the Gothic atmosphere of the French Renaissance, with its chateau-style inspired spires and steeply pitched roof. Detective Barrett led Wilmot and Foley inside, where they were met by the tearful look on Coby's face—sat on a backless bench. She dried her eyes. Her gaze fluttered about the room, as if she had not seen them. As they passed her, Foley stopped to offer his condolences. Wilmot backtracked to hear them. "How are you holding up in these trying times?" asked Foley.

"Thank you for your kind words," said Coby. She sighed. Her head fell into her hands, then rose with a flushed complexion. "I'm doing well, considering the circumstances." Her raddled voice came out harsh and coarse. "I just can't believe this is happening. It doesn't feel real."

Wilmot entered Coby's eyeline. She recoiled at his presence. "I assure you," said Wilmot, "this is no fantasy." He looked down upon her, with his arms akimbo.

Coby rolled her eyes. "What do you know about what's real?" she asked. "You couldn't even fathom an asexual relationship between two women. You were questioning my marriage from the moment we met."

"Considering you sought out our services," said Wilmot, "I believe the same could be said for you."

"How dare you?" Coby gave Detective Barrett a dirty look. "What did you bring them here for? To insult me?"

"Excuse us, Mrs. Triggs," said Detective Barrett. He wrangled in Wilmot and Foley, then shoved them in the direction of his office. "I was just bringing these gentlemen in for routine questioning." On his way inside, he offered her a humble bow of the head. "I apologize on their behalf."

"I should think so," said Coby. Her eyes followed Wilmot into the office with a scornful grimace. "At least someone around here has some manners."

Beyond the lighted door was a cubicle farm of partner desks. Detective Barrett carted Wilmot and Foley through the bustle of cops and their latest batch of patsies, until the trio made their way to his desk. He gestured for them to take a seat, then dumped a file on Emery's case in front of them.

They flipped through the information. A series of photographs, taken of Emery and Blythe, caught their attention. Foley brought the picture up to his eye. He gave the once over to every pixel and pel. His lips parted in a wide-eyed gape. He gave this treatment to each image on the table, then drew in his breath at a sharp intake. These were his photographs—the ones he took of Emery and Blythe for Coby. "I don't understand," he said. "How would Blythe have these?"

Wilmot leered at Coby's silhouette in the opaque tempered glass in the office window. His exhales permeated the air in swirls of vaporized nicotine. "She wouldn't," he said, "but I think I have an idea of who would."

Foley loosed an acrid look at Wilmot. Detective Barrett shared his apprehension.

Once more, Detective Barrett stepped through the lighted door. He poked his head out into the hall. "Coby," he said, "could you come here for a second?"

Coby strolled in. She presented, before them, as a mousy muggins. Her eyeline danced around the room until it landed upon Detective Barrett as its swing partner. "Yes," she said, "what seems to be the problem?"

Wilmot crowed. "You're a killer," he said. "That's the problem."

In her stance, her posture straightened and her knees locked into place. She dug in her heels, firm in her resolve. "I'm afraid I have no idea what you're referring to," she said. "If you'd like we can give my lawyer a call, since you're so keen on throwing around wild accusations."

Wilmot snapped. His footfalls barreled toward her at a swift rate and, in his loafers, each step landed with a heavy *thud*. He stopped mere inches from her. "I'm afraid you know exactly what we're referring to and, I'm sure, you're afraid we've caught on to your little game." He pushed the loose stack of photographs in her face. "Look at those pictures." His eyebrows raised. "Do they look familiar to you?"

She flinched. Her lips puckered, in a subtle cringe. Then, she took a beat and regained her composure. "I haven't the slightest clue what you're going on about."

"Oh," he said, "that's right, because you don't get your hands dirty, do you? You just let others handle your dirty work for you. That's why you hired Foley in the first place. You wanted him to find you your get out of marriage for free card, but it wasn't so simple. Was it? So, you manipulate your own wife into committing murder on your behalf. Isn't that right?"

"This is preposterous," she said. "You can't actually believe that." Her doe eyes brimmed with tears. She looked to those around her for support. "Are you just going to let him berate me like this?"

Foley averted his gaze. Detective Barrett did likewise.

Wilmot strode back and forth between partner desks. "I've seen some sloppy kills in my day," he said, "but using our photos to blackmail your wife to commit murder." He sucked his teeth. "That has to take the cake." He cracked a wry smirk. "I mean you could've at least edited them a bit. With the filters and apps they've got nowadays it should've been a cinch." His pacing came to a halt. He turned to her, face-to-face. "I've got to hand it to you though. No matter what, Emery's still facing first degree murder and the most you'll get is a solicitation of murder for hire charge." He shook his head. "Mission accomplished, I'd say."

Coby bit her bottom lip. Her fingers fiddled with the rings on her hands. She closed her eyes. When she opened them again, it was as if they were speaking to a new woman altogether. The privileged demeanor was traded in for a shattered self-image. "Fine," she said, "I admit it. I sent the blackmail under Blythe's name." Muscles tensed around her jawline. "Emery thought she was so clever—playing her little games behind my back, with God knows who, knowing I couldn't do a thing about it until I proved her wrongdoings in court." Her hands balled to closed fists upon her lap. "That damn prenup was airtight. She made sure of that." She gritted her teeth. "Well, I knew something she could never admit to herself." She rolled up a sleeve on her vicuna turtleneck sweater and revealed fresh bruises on her arm. "I know how Emery will always resort to violence when cornered." There was a lull, as she stared out into the ether of an equivocal universe. "You see, there's a stipulation in our prenup. Neither of us can commit a felony above the fourth degree." She shrugged. "I figured this was it, my only way out. Like dominoes, I set her up and watch her fall." She looked down at her feet. "That was the idea anyway." A chilling laughter bubbled to the surface. "Emery always claimed ours was a marriage of convenience," she said, "in the end, I suppose I proved her right."

Her hysterics broke into sobs.

Foley traipsed over to Coby. His eyes met hers with solace. He rested a hand on her shoulder. "At least, now, you'll finally be free from Emery's iron grip," he told her.

Wilmot sniggered. "And we'll be free of yours."

Detective Barrett placed Coby in restraints and rattled off her rights in an ambivalent tone. She was off-loaded into the booking room to have her fingerprint taken. Her eyes cast downward, and her tail tucked between her legs.

Wilmot and Foley bid the precinct farewell and stepped out onto the city street. Wilmot sighed. He gave his partner a sideways look. "That was an exciting afternoon," he said. Foley nodded. "What do you think? Should we take the rest of the day off, paint the town red?" He offered a nervous smile. "I could take you out to eat, you know, like a proper date." His hooded eyes widened, full of dire anticipation.

Foley's forehead creased. He found himself nodding before the question even registered. "Yeah," he said, "I'd love that." His lips peeled back in a crooked grin. "There's a nice Mediterranean place a couple blocks from here that I've been meaning to try."

Wilmot achieved a newfound bounce in his step. His parted lips unveiled a devilish smile. He placed a guiding hand on the small of Foley's back that crept lower as they walked. He leaned in, to Foley's tousled bedhead, and said, "Lead the way."

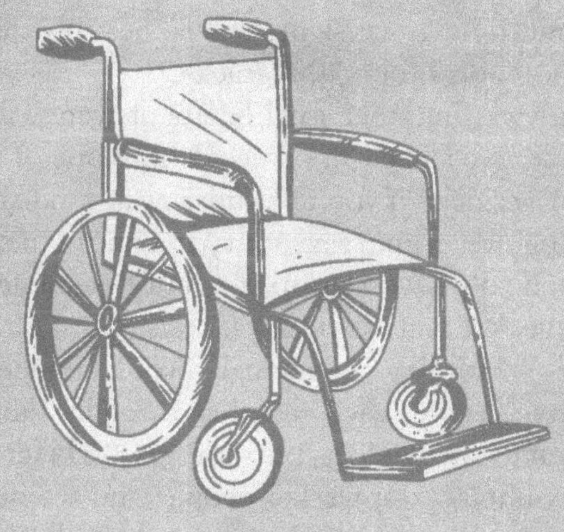

Revenge of the Wild Wheeled Werebutch
Alex Liddell

First things first, we remember everything we do as wolves. The idea we all black out when we wolf out is bullshit. It's just a lot easier to explain ourselves when we get caught, helps certain people sleep easier with what we do.

In fact, I think my memory has improved since I got bit. The stuff about all your senses getting enhanced is true; sight, smell, hearing, feeling, memory too I think, that tracks.

Anyway, another total lie about werewolves is the idea we all get bit on accident. None of us get bit by accident, if you're wandering around at night hoping for some sexy out of control beast to scratch you, I won't stop you, but I guarantee you will die. We will eat you.

It's nothing personal you understand, werewolves vet each member carefully the same reason the mafia does, the same reason biker gangs and vampires do; we kill people, and we need to make damn sure nobody goes to the police.

That's what I learnt, it doesn't matter if you have a moral code or ground rules or status, in the end you're killing people, for fun. That requires careful planning and secrecy, because that operation can be easily fucked up by just one person.

I know this, because in my first pack, I was the person who fucked everything up, technically.

I did go in knowing and accepting the bloodshed and hair growth, and don't get it twisted, I do not regret becoming who I am. But it's just, well, in retrospect, I was introduced to it in a way that is designed to cause problems. My girlfriend introduced me, my now ex-girlfriend.

We met on a Pride night at a bar called Bambi's. I broke away from the friends I came in with, I just dropped everything, practically breaking the toes of anybody who wouldn't move out the way immediately like an excited puppy, just to ask her about her arm tattoos.

She had this winged timber wolf drawn in blackwork that's leaping up her bicep with an anatomically correct heart in its mouth, and it's flying into a vortex that looks a lot like a moon surrounded by stars. So cool.

Her arms were, very muscular. I tapped on one, she turned around, and she didn't scan the room above my head like every abled person does when first meeting me, expecting some "normal" to look back at their eyeline. She, looked directly at me, and smiled.

I can put that down to her enhanced senses mapping me before I even slid over to her. That didn't make it less romantic when I found that out though. She was waiting for me to make the first move, and she was happy that I had made it. She could feel every hair follicle on me stand to attention as I gently poked her.

Thinking about it now, she absolutely knew she had me before I even knew how deeply I wanted her. And damn, as soon as she opened her mouth to explain every tattoo she had on her body and the story behind them, I wanted her so, so deeply.

I buy her drinks; she buys me drinks. Next thing I know I've told her my entire life story up until the second I saw her, and she's curled up on my lap, her strong arm wrapped around the back of my neck for balance, her opposite hand stroking the bristles of my undercut.

That was the first and last time I've ever let anybody sit on me. I didn't know what to think of it because I wasn't thinking. It felt good to not think or care about anything except balancing this beautiful drunk woman on me as she whispered happy nonsense into my ear. Doesn't that just sum it up?

When the pub's kick-out time came, we agreed upon our first kiss that we'd kill everyone in the world and burn together in their funeral pyre just to ensure that nobody would ever come between us, and we sealed that promise with tongue. I didn't even ask her name, I found out it was Becca because it was above the phone number she wrote down.

We moved in together four weeks later. Yes, a very healthy relationship, glad you agree.

In our defence (her defence more than mine), she waited a year to drop the bomb that she was a werewolf and she wanted to make me part of her womyn's murder club from the moment we got together. I was a little upset at first, but we spent the whole day and night talking and I agreed that this was the best way for her to vet me and trust her. If she wasn't sure things would work out, she'd gently remove herself from my life.

And besides, if she told me that when we first got together, I would have politely declined her offer thinking that she was some kind of weirdo who wanted to roleplay with her polycule or something. No judgement if you're into that, it's just not my jam.

And while she was convinced that I was her life mate and born to be a lunar lesbian like her, she also had to convince her pack that I was the perfect fit. That took a year of observation apparently, which normally would ring alarm bells. However, I did accept that at the time, they had to be sure I wouldn't blab or have a complete mental breakdown, right? That seems reasonable under the circumstances.

And, well, I loved her, deeply. I didn't need to trust any of her friends who had been monitoring our private life for the past year, I just needed to trust her, and I did. I do not recommend doing that.

Anyway, the point is nobody is turned immediately into a werewolf, not just because of all the reasons I said, the process itself takes a while. There's a lot of prep work and after care, and when it happens it hurts, a lot.

How do I put this? The process involves biting, and it's hard for us to "hold back" when it comes to biting. There is a chance that introducing a new friend to the fold becomes a feeding frenzy. So, to minimise the chances of that happening, there's a mandatory introduction period where the pack "gets their scent on you".

That means months of scheduled introductions and "activities" designed to give you a sneak peek of your new life, as well as establishing emotional ties that will hopefully sink into the muscle memory of your new besties.

What this means, I'm told, varies among packs, but for ours it was a lot of strange and sudden camping trips. It was painfully ordinary mostly, the seven of us sharing stories and feelings in the woods.

There was Nancy, who looked the oldest, but I never asked how old. I was told she had a wife somewhere, who still doesn't know what our secret camping trips were about.

Probably the youngest was Jenni, who talked the most about gender politics and other things I pretended to understand and care about. I mostly remember her for her long rants on who the most ethical targets for the hunts were and why lesbian separatists shouldn't eat penises, as if that was the most important thing in the world to anybody besides herself.

Gail was a tattooist, she did Becca's awesome arm tattoo, allegedly that's how they met but I sometimes felt they had sex once upon a time. I did hang out with her the most out of all of them though, she was alright.

Quin worked in a pharmacy, which is how we all got free illegal and often necessary medical supplies. I highly recommend having a Quin in a pack, incredibly useful. She was dating Jenni, who went to the same university as her and was who introduced her to the pack, so they kept telling me.

Emily had a van and played guitar, she didn't reveal more than that to me, it was clear she didn't like me from the start. I think she was my favourite overall, at least she was honest in everything she did, good musician too.

Then there was Becca, the gorgeous one. And me, the awkward one who took a long time being lifted out of the van and mostly asked silly questions that got vague answers, who just nodded along most nights.

For around six months, my entire life was just listening to them and watching them and telling them how excited I was to be there. It was tolerable because it was all building up to me turning and living a happy life with Becca and her divine wolf sisters.

The best part of that very dull period was when I got to watch them lure a birdwatching group into the disused camping ground we used, which Jenni kept telling me she all vetted for having terrible politics and loathsome personalities. They put me in a nature hide that was chained shut and I got to watch the whole show like a giggling creep.

I have to wonder if that was their way of trying to freak me out, maybe the final straw to break me, but I passed their freak test with flying colours. I really wish they let me film it, they completely obliterated those nature nerds, it was hilarious.

The anticipation of the twitchers setting up camp for an early start to catch a glimpse of the lesser spotted cock bird or whatever they were told, followed by rustling in the undergrowth, then a tornado of blood, fur and bobble hats.

While Nancy and Quin stayed with the first corpses to munch away the evidence, Gail and Emily ran after the smarter members of the group who heard the rustling and started running before the pounce. They did not get far.

And I'm not sure if this was intended to this day, but Becca was able to chase one of the poor nerds back to camp, gave him a little hope, then she fell from the sky to pin him to the ground where I swear his intestines came out his mouth like a tube of toothpaste making a sound like a wet whoopee cushion.

She nearly fell out a thirty-foot pine tree to pull that off, legendary.

I was glowing when they unlocked the hide. I was ready, they all knew it, so it was decided I would be turned the next week. I was doing donuts around the camp that was muddy with liquidised birdwatchers.

Now this is a bit embarrassing, I'm not saying all turnings go this way, this is just how it was done with me. I did a few practice runs with Becca, with some special clamps she had from when she was preparing to be turned, the less said about that the better. And they made me write a plausible suicide note in case things went south; I was convinced we wouldn't need it.

Basically, you're laid naked on a table, tied down tight. You don't need to be naked, but your clothes will be ruined if you're not. There's a bit of weed smoking beforehand, so everyone was chill. Becca put on an ambient music playlist for me, which chilled everyone out some more. The gals wolf out and circle around you slowly, sniffing you out, maybe licking a bit. Then one by one, each shewolf bites down on a body part.

Gail was first, she latched onto the right side of my stomach, just hard enough to break the skin and get those sweet lycan juices into me.

Quin and Jenni each took a leg, which they seemed to have no restraint over knowing that I didn't use them, which I was a little annoyed they assumed but had no time to think about it as Nancy clamped her teeth on my right forearm.

Now that did hurt, that made me wince back tears, but I was determined not to kill the vibe. Looking back, I wish we had discussed what bits I was most comfortable with being bitten, I wish I discussed a lot more things if I'm honest. But I was so focussed on doing this, on getting to be them, I just shut my mouth and let it happen, they knew best.

I did scream a little when Emily took my entire boob in her mouth, which killed the vibe for me. But as planned I just readjusted and let the saliva do its magic.

Becca took my left shoulder, where I needed her to be to get through it all. I just looked into her giant yellow eye as she wriggled her jaw deeper. I swear I could feel teeth touch bone, but I got through it by focussing on her soothing, rumbling growls.

Anyway, I lost a lot of blood in the process, which is normal. I passed out a short while after it was done, also normal.

I opened my eyes and two days had passed, the bite marks had disappeared, closed up and healed as if nothing happened, it was working.

Becca was at the foot of my bed rubbing my belly when I woke up, they'd all been taking turns watching me. They'd stashed me in a cabin at the disused campgrounds and all stayed the nights I was asleep; they did the room up really nice for me with balloons and everything. Happy birthday to new me.

I was a mess. I was crying and laughing and eating furiously in bed. Becca curled around me, I kissed, licked and nuzzled her and we had the best sex we've ever had, everything was enhanced and important now. Every touch, taste and smell was available to us and it was working, oh my god it was working.

Then after a nap, I wake up, and the first thing I hear is: "why isn't it working?"

I woke up a little more, I definitely heard Becca say: "everyone takes their own time, she'll fully turn eventually."

I was turned, what does she mean? In my sleepy state I focussed my ears, I shift them around like antenna and discover that I was tuning in the voices from outside my cabin, far outside my cabin. Why were they that far outside?

"I took three days," said Quin, "she might take longer given her condition."

What condition? Oh no, please, no.

"And if she doesn't? What then?" I could taste the spit from Jenni as she said that, "have you even tried getting her out of bed?"

"She's been too busy eating her out to try that."

Fuck you.

"Yes, very funny Gail, this is serious. Let's face it, every bit of her has healed except the one thing that needs to be healed, it isn't working."

Fuck you, Jenni.

"How is it not working? Turning fixed my back problems and all her bite marks are gone, maybe she just needs a little push out the pram to get her going."

Fuck you, Emily.

"Well, if we are going to undo all of this, we have to decide soon otherwise she'll be stuck in that state, we'll be stuck with her like that."

Fuck you, Nancy.

"I have to agree, we did say if something went wrong, we'd act fast, we planned for this, we only have a short window to inject her. I don't want to have to kill her, but it might be better than leaving her like that."

Fuck you, Quin.

"Okay will everyone just chill please, she just needs more time, I didn't press the issue, but I will, okay? She probably just hasn't tried it yet. She's not used to it-"

Don't fucking say it Becca, shut up shut up.

"I'll go back in there and teach her to walk if I have to, she'll use her legs tonight."

FUCK YOU BECCA.

The time it took for her to walk to my cabin was enough time for me to think about and rethink everything in my miserable life. I really don't recommend having an anxiety attack with werewolf blood pumping in you, that truly felt like I was dying, I wanted to rip off all my skin and eat it.

I left my old life, my old friends behind to do this, I put all my savings and future into this relationship, and like an idiot I didn't see this coming. I went over every conversation I've ever had with these bitches, everything suddenly became so crystal clear it blinded me in a white-hot rage.

Of course, that's why they put my chair in the car before the ritual, they thought I wasn't going to need it again. All those jokes they made about Becca not having to carry me anymore, I thought it was because my arms would be strong enough to carry her, but oh no, I just didn't get the joke. I didn't get that I was a joke that they were going to make serious.

All those arguments about helping me replace my wheelchair for a better model, telling me to wait until after I was turned. Becca wasn't worried about me changing sizes, she was expecting for me to never use a chair again.

God, I just wanted to turn so bad, to be with Becca so bad, I shut out all the obvious questions to keep the vibe going. Well, that vibe was stone dead now.

I didn't do this to be "cured" of myself, even if it was possible, I wouldn't choose it, I just wanted to be a werewolf. I wanted Becca to know that I already had a plan to commission a bigger wheelchair, with spikes and chains that could keep speed with me and smash open doors and support us both. We'd entrap some rich bastards in the camp and take their bank details so we wouldn't need the money, we'd have enough time. We'd work things out if we just talked.

We can't just throw it all away over this one little thing, right? I wanted to tell her that if carrying me bothered her so much she didn't have to, I'd carry myself.

I didn't manage to get this across to her in the middle of a nervous breakdown. I could just get out "fuck you" as I scratched her stupid pretty face as soon as she hovered over me.

Everything was suddenly overwhelming and incomprehensible. All I could do was scream, flail at Becca who demanded I let her hold me up, and eventually I'd piss the bed out of spite. The only thing I achieved was getting dumped on the floor as the rest of them rushed in for damage control.

I only remember the first few blows to my face and the needle going into my neck. I open my eyes and I'm in hospital, I shout for a nurse, and she tells me I'm going to be transferred to a special ward now I'm conscious. The special ward had suicide watches and special counsellors; I'd have to be signed off by them before I could leave. I really needed mental help, this was serious, and manipulative to do this just after a bad break up. I was very lucky that my friends found me when I tried to throw myself off a hill, it could've been fatal.

My friends. My divine wolf sisters. They'd thrown me down the stairs and expected me to get up. Then they just left me when I didn't. They didn't even have the decency to kill me, and it turned out they didn't have the courage to visit me either.

I assumed the shot they gave me was a mix of silver nitrate, wolfsbane and tranquilizers. That's how you can stop someone turning, but you have to stick someone with it soon after they get bit, before they've had their first real kill, otherwise it's useless.

I figured that's why my neck was the only part of my body that still hurt. But you never really know if the cocktail has worked until there's a reason to wolf out and nothing happens.

And you know what the scariest part is? I might never had known if it worked if I didn't transfer wards.

The nurse assigned to me wheeled me into the elevator, even if I knew where I was going, I was too depressed to move my arms, so I just let her push me and drone on about her life and how much better I'd be after this journey. Déjà vu.

It was on the fourth floor, we were on the first, the doors opened on the second and this dude, wearing a baby blue tracksuit and holding some cheap perfume from the giftshop, crams himself in with us.

Dude was clearly a visitor and neither knew or cared that the elevator only supports one wheelchair and two and a half people, he is providing a half too much and his groin is pressed against my shoulder.

Nobody says anything. He sighs, he fidgets, he grunts and sniffs and clears his throat, his breath stinks of canteen lasagne, and he smiles at the nurse then me.

I begin to feel an emotion different to depression, and as that rises within me, I start to smell the cheap perfume inside the bottle. It's sickly and chemical, it's so strong that he might as well have poured it directly into my mouth. I smell his sweat pumping out his pores seeping into his tracksuit, I hear his veins pulsating, I see his meat and cheese laden breath seep out of his jellied lungs, up his throat, from behind his gold fillings and he says:

"Would you mind moving a bit luv?"

My nurse doesn't start screaming until his head flops onto her shoulder and lies there for a good few seconds as the remaining skin tears away from his neck and separates from the rest of his body, her mind isn't quick enough to process what has happened. We both start to panic, but I am faster and now taking up most of the elevator space, the dude's body sinks to the floor spurting blood and perfume everywhere and I puked right then and there all over us.

Nursie was pinned with the back of my chair and scrambling like a mouse in a glue trap, and I do the only thing that makes sense at the time. I use my claws to pull myself up to face her, and I bite her face off. I chew quickly, and swallow, then I collapse unconscious on all that filth pooling in this tiny metal box.

I woke up for the second time in a hospital bed and I'm in shock, or so the doctors tell me. Apparently, we all made it to the fourth floor and mentally scarred a few student doctors for life as this sea of vomit, blood, hair and twisted metal gushed onto their shoes when the doors opened.

After that ordeal, me having mixed emotions was an understatement. I was going out of my mind feeling hysterically happy that my gift hadn't been taken from me, and hysterically scared that the police were waiting to talk to me.

For a good few minutes, I thought the world was ending. That was until the female officer said:

"can you give us a description of the thing that attacked you?"

I was still frozen up, but as luck would have it, they all interpreted that as me being too traumatised to talk.

"This… thing… it wasn't human… I know this is hard, but can you remember anything that happened in the elevator?"

I stared blankly at her trained sympathetic expression, it's that familiar pity that everyone from social workers to shopkeepers give me. The "oh you poor thing, your legs are useless, you've been through so much" look. But this time, instead of hating that look, it cleared the cobwebs in my mind.

My god, I thought, she doesn't think I did that. She doesn't think I could've done that because I'm in a chair. She doesn't think werewolves come in wheelchairs, oh my god, I'm in the clear!

While fireworks are going off in my head, I simply commit to staring at the cop with tears pooling in my eyes and that's enough for her to consider me a lost cause. She puts her card down on the side table and thanks me for my time.

I hear her clearly in the distance say, "poor thing, what kind of monster attacks a girl in a wheelchair?" And I allow myself a big old smile behind the bed curtains, because the whole world opened up to me.

Before, there was all this prep work put into hunts, stuff that I hoped the others would continue to organise, because I sure can't be arsed.

All this deception and stalking, trying to find the perfect victims who most definitely deserve to be killed and won't be missed? I don't need to do any of that, I don't need to think about any of that, nobody thinks a girl in a wheelchair is going to tear them to shreds, that's it.

I've left tire tracks all over the piles of meat I've run into, I've gone back to crime scenes to revisit my handiwork, sometimes with blood on my lips, I'm invisible. It's been seventy-four kills, one of which was a few streets away from my home, and I've never even been questioned by police. No kidding.

I found out, quite simply, that you can't win a fist fight in an enclosed space with a rabid dog, even without their hind legs they have their front claws and their jaws. And it's especially easy to push someone into a corner when they're trying to help you back out of that corner.

I supposed that's not very noble, but like I said, the main thing is being practical, and everyone's very bad assumptions has turned out to be very practical for me.

It was especially practical in getting each member of my old pack alone to have a little chat about what happened. I still can't believe they thought they could take me by themselves, it's almost unfair.

I didn't even have to come to Jenni, she came to my house about killing Emily. Oh yeah, I killed Emily a week before Jenni came to visit, it was just a spur of the moment thing. I figured it would be funny if I cut her breaks, which would ruin the plans of the whole group for their little camping trips. I had a whole speech prepared where I'd watch her crawl from the wreckage and say like "how's that for a push out the pram EMILY?"

But she couldn't get her seatbelt off, and I think she had a concussion because she didn't wolf out and was slurring her words, not really registering what was happening, so I just pulled myself into the passenger seat and eviscerated her without a word between us. This is why I don't prepare speeches, it's just a waste.

Anyway, Jenni got her own speech prepared and stormed in to give it to me, blah blah blah "I always knew you couldn't handle it" something, something "I know what you did and you'll pay for it" yadda, yadda "you're weak, you're nothing, you can't win in a real fight" boring boring shut up.

Funny story, the next day I had to explain to my very concerned neighbour the concept of "goodbye sex", which is not a conversation you want to have with an eighty-year-old who just wrapped her head around lesbianism existing.

There was just so much noise she was worried if me and Becca had a fight and if I was okay.

I said that we'd broken up, but we had some goodbye angry sex which really gave us closure to our intense relationship and we were both very okay and the break up was mutual and we both had a very good very loud final time together and unfortunately she just left but I'll tell her that you said hi next time we meet as friends in future I'm sorry to worry you Mrs Perkins okay bye now!

Not my finest moment but the upside was she completely avoided me from then on, so I was able to burn the remains of Jenni in the little shared back garden in a bin without any eyes on me. There wasn't much left, just her shoes and bag, I kept the money, cards and family pictures in her purse.

Killing her was annoying, my chair got dented permanently when I threw it at her stupid fluffy face, I had to spend a lot of her money to replace it. But she was in my house, I know where all the tough corners are, and it was easy to push her into one after she got blindsided by a wheelchair to the face. That's one of my favourite moves, nobody expects it, I'd do it more often but, well, it's expensive and risky.

After Jenni's disappearance I got a tearful call from Quin telling me the gals want to talk things over, I tell her and the gals to go fuck themselves they know where to find me, just like how Jenni knew how to find me.

I'm actually still in touch with Quin as it happens, she wisely stayed out of the drama after that, when I ask her for something she gets it without hassle, it's always good to have a Quin around, she's a good girl.

Anyway, Nancy of all people tries to jump me a while later when I'm on my way home from a New Years Eve party, and I have to give her credit she beat the shit out of me. I was tipsy, I missed the last bus, I didn't want to argue with cab drivers, so I thought fuck it, I can defend myself at night alone. That's stupid even for a werewolf, don't do like I did.

She threw me out of my chair after she jumped on me from the roof of a Chinese takeaway, before I could even process that, I hit a brick wall, and she began using me as her personal chew toy. It was brutal, if I had time to think I'd have thought it was the end, I saw what my pancreas looked like that night.

With Nancy it was just a case of wearing her down, she always did pounces like this and stayed to eat what was already killed because, although she'd never say it like this, she lacked stamina. All I had to do was not die before she ran out of breath, and despite her smashing my face into concrete to turn my brains into hamburger, I heard her breath starting to get shallow.

The only part of me that wasn't throbbing and useless was the claw on my right index finger, Nancy lunged her head down for the fatal bite to the head, and by some miracle I hit a vein in her jugular and clung onto that wound like a tape worm. She hurled me about like ragdoll on a washing line, but I didn't let go until she completely bled out with my nail twisting the vein open wide.

That was rough, it seemed to take forever to drain all the wolf out of her until this empty old woman was all that was left. I just left her pale and naked in a pile of rubbish bags behind the takeaway, dragged myself to my chair and then home, I passed out in the bathroom. Not untypical of someone returning home from a New Years Party, so again, I got no questions.

I did later read that the cops tried to blame Nancy's wife for her murder if you can believe that. The idea that two lesbian pensioners would argue over mysterious camping trips and leave one naked and dead in an alley hundreds of miles from their bungalow, you have to laugh right?

I knew Becca would send Gail after me, she didn't have the stones to text me let alone kill me, and I knew that I'd pissed too far on their parade. But let me be clear here, I actually liked Gail, I didn't want to kill her, but you have to be practical when dealing with intercommunity fighting okay?

I healed up almost overnight from Nancy's thorough arse kicking, but I'm not an idiot, I'm not going to let anybody get the jump on me again because I may not be so lucky. In a way, getting the drop on Gail was self-defence, she never got the chance to surprise me.

And to be honest, if the tattoo parlour installed ramps, if they didn't make Gail lock up late every night, if they didn't cheap out on security cameras, I wouldn't have had to crawl from the back door to the break room just to sneak up on her and chew off her femoral arteries.

So, when you think about it, her workplace caused this more than anything, I didn't enjoy doing that as much as I enjoyed swallowing her whole. I had to unhinge my jaw for that one, that was neat.

That got Becca's attention, finally. She didn't have anybody to hide behind or distract her anymore. And of course, there would be that awkward moment where she'd try to fight me, reason with me, or God forbid, try to get back together with me.

I didn't expect her to run. That really hurt. This incredible, beautiful, confident, deadly timber wolf who ate my heart and spat it out, who I would've died for, who said she would die for me, who we agreed would kill everyone in our way to stay together just texted me "I'm leaving town, congrats on ruining everything, don't come after me."

I guess all we had was bullshit. I have to laugh, after everything we went through, she really thought a text would stop me.

That's when I discovered I could get up to sixty miles per hour if I took the road instead of the pavement. What little traffic did see this hairy hulk squeezed into a wheelchair and crop top skating across the icy tarmac didn't report it. Some probably booked a therapy session or two.

She was at the old campground packing some old shit into a hire car, I guess she'd been living there since she moved out. I actually felt her heart fall down to her arse, no kidding, the body is a miraculous instrument.

Now don't get it twisted, I'm nice really, and if I'm honest I do still feel a little something for her. You don't get out easily from such a special relationship like that.

I wanted to say so much to her, I wanted her to hurt, I wanted to calmly explain that we needed to communicate our needs better, I wanted to pull out each of her ribs one by one, I wanted to kiss her and apologise and explain the circumstances, I said nothing and neither did she.

When she was standing there, feeling fear for the first time in years, tears and sweat pulsating out of her with each heartbeat, all I could think to say was "I can carry you now."

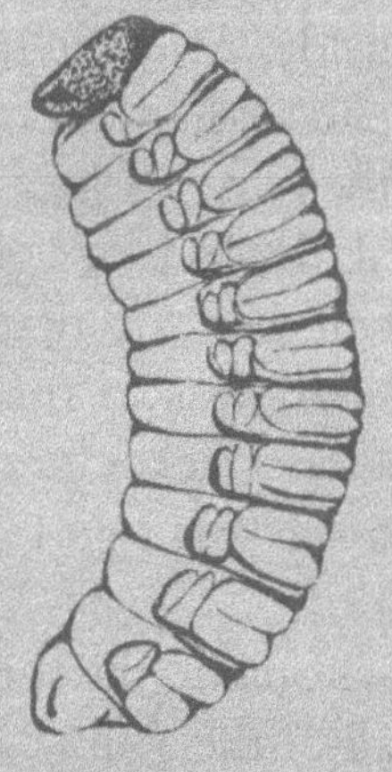

Mr. Grub

Sergio "ente per ente" Palumbo

It was long after darkness had wrapped the whole street outside when the three youngsters eventually had entered unseen, being waring. Their exploration of the building did not prove to be very fruitful, and meager was their contentment for the few valuable things found and gloatingly apprehended so far. Then, they spotted the other door in the distance, and there was nothing that could stop them from getting to that and watching what else was inside. After all, they had come here for a reason, and didn't like to think they had almost wasted that whole night.

Once opened, the lack of light continued to be the main characteristic of that house, even past that door. The darkness in the unknown area of the building being thicker and darker than the ground floor it was cold and dark as hell down here!

Shoulder-to-shoulder, the three young ones had reached the head of the stairs before starting to go down, while attentively moving through the darkness that filled the place, their flashlight being the only means to safely open a way ahead. They had kept unceasingly walking like a small vessel that dared sail through that matter that that looked like a black lake. Or even, going on, not differently from a mophead of dark curls invisibly waving in the dead of the night. It went all the way down to be followed to the desired target being uncertain, and not without possible dangers.

That sequence of steps was taking them into the unknown, in a way.

But the thing they had found in the end wasn't what they might have ever expected, and the consequences of their moves, and their decisions, of today proved to be more unbelievable than they could have ever imagined. Though, it couldn't be changed by now. Nothing might be forgotten…There was no hope at all that it might be all be a very bad dream. It was not anything they could remove from their mind as if it had never happened, or had never been real.

Because the fear they felt was a real thing, and the bad outcome of their night a sad fact, undoubtedly.

This city really should be to everyone's satisfaction, all the people who had lived in, or had visited, Seattle thought so of this modern urban area. Having been renamed in the 1800safter the Native American Chief Sealth, who helped in removing violent tensions between colonizers and local tribes, and being located on the shore of a sparkling and wide bay with the snowy peak of Mount Rainier in the distance and a modern skyline of glass skyscrapers. Surely, Seattle had a famously and world-renowned setting. Was there somebody that didn't know of this place, its historic buildings, the great view tourists might have from the observation deck of its 605-ft-tall characteristic landmark from the 1962World Fair – the Space Age-modernist city tower-like structure supported by three curved steel legs – that was most appealing at night when it was lit up, and hadn't ever be overwhelmed by the really spectacular sceneries that you could see in Washington State? Probably not... Its downtown was full of coffeehouses, many restaurants and engaging clubs, making a lengthy visit worthwhile, especially during the summer.

This was even the part of the Pacific Northwest of America where the legends recounted that Coyote – the contradictory, and colorful male figure of all the ancient Native American cultural traditions –had built waterfalls, long ago, in several Washington rivers to keep fishes from reaching areas inhabited by people who refused his attentions toward their beautiful women. The part of the country where several mountains, lakes, and rivers were also identified in local myths dating back to the oldest times; and then, here the shamans had been feared for many and many centuries because of the supernatural power they were reputed to be endowed with but were regarded as a necessary part of the Native communities because of their ability to mediate between Mankind and the spirit world. Some of them were also able to do battle with the *kushtakas* to reclaim the soul of someone in danger, or thought to have been lost at sea. This, without forgetting about the many fabled tales of the Raven as a trickster…

Of course, Seattle wasn't just made of its great sceneries and its modern downtown, there were also the outskirts of the urban area, from the more established and costly neighborhoods to the University District, and then, from there to its less attractive—and more distant—commuter belt as it was called by the so-called suburbanites that stayed there, who went day-by-day trying to survive.

Mr. Grub lived in one of those houses on a hilltop just off the southern road, one of those places where wealthy men rarely visited and much more rarely they bought a house for themselves.

Actually, Grub wasn't his true name, but the locals had started calling him that about 10 years ago. 'This term of abuse implied that he looked like a short, fat burrowing invertebrate animal with a long soft body that could be spotted in the ground. The more common term was Mr. Grub among the boys like Hernández, but you had to pay attention not to say that name to his face when you stumbled into him while going along the street – and it might occur at times…though it was frequent to be whispering that word referred to him just when you got past him, or stayed at his back. …Of course, Mr. Grub was an object of derision and he usually was made fun of both from any child or a grown-up boy in that area. It seemed to be because he walked with much difficulty, but there was no one among the neighbors who knew his real name. how he really was named. Even on his front door, or letterbox, there was no name anymore, and this because Mr. Grub was about 80when he came here to live. From that moment on he had immediately displayed his lack of interest in what the others could think of him, nor cared he for what they might say about his slovenly way of life. He left his small garden not well cleaned, as it was always full of leaves and dead herbs, nor did much for the outside of his house. People thought that inside those walls – where nobody ever entered, or so they said anyway…it might be even worse…

Less than 6ft tall, an uncertain gait that characterized his walk in the open, and a short neck. He talked—the few times he was heard to say something—in a strange and very toilful way, as if he had a sort of invisible knife between his teeth. The dark eyes on his wrinkled face that gave him a slumberous look appeared to be always tired, or really distracted for most of the day, as if he had seen in his long life more things than those he liked to remember, and certainly more interesting facts than what he could spot in that distant and mainly moneyless area of the city where he lived now. The big, crumpled nose that was the most prominent of his features seemed to be a ruined outcrop about to suddenly fall down from a bigger rock, his hair was whitish, at least the few curls he had on his almost completely bald head had that color…Well, not much of an attractive man, if he had ever been so during his younger age, of course. But who could say so…?

Many thought that Mr. Grub was not only very old now, but he was also ill, and that he already was ill when he first came to stay here. Well, nobody knew what illness it might be, but he seemed to have long been affected by it. Actually, though bad that condition happened to be, he was still in this world, and apart his trembling legs, and his slowness of motion, he didn't appear to be almost going to die very soon. As the common saying went, *also the oldest quitch was die-hard*…It had to be said that, even if that illness was bad, whatever it might be, it had allowed him to live until today, and that meant for ten years after he had decided to live in that untidied house of his.

Too many hearsays, and bad images were around about Mr. Grub: some thought he was a vampire—but, no, vampires were all young, and powerful, at least this was how they looked like in the movies, Hernández had replied to his friends…and even that all he showed off about him was a false appearance, just to deceive everyone. But didn't vampires walk outside only at night as they were afraid of the Sun…? Actually, as

Mr. Grub went out for buying food during the morning, this obviously ruled out that improbable occurrence. Others considered him to be only a bilker that had made it all just to get the money he received every month posing as a disabled person, while he felt good. Well, Hernández doubted also it. Why walking like a cripple every day out of the house, to reach the garden, or to enter the food store, just like that? Well, some would say it was for the money, and that was surely a good reason, at least one that Hernández could imagine was comprehensible. But in his heart the 16-year-old boy with long chestnut curls thought it wasn't so, he didn't know why he said it, but he felt that really in that man there was something that didn't go well. And it might be only because of some illness they hadn't identified yet. Nor that he, or others, really cared, of course.

But this had nothing to do with what the three, Hernández, Guyader and Jouna, had on their mind.

The reality, though sad, was that probably he was an old man all the others had simply forgotten, and he had nobody else still around who could look after him. This might be of help to the three in what they had planned to do, and it meant bad things to Mr. Grub anyway.

As it wasn't just because the three young ones had an interest in that old man that they kept an eye on his moves, but it was what his house could have inside that was of importance: after all, some among them had thought, if he was a retired person and had bought that house, he had to have some money, maybe even some objects which could be very valuable, and be sold very easily to someone, once taken and properly dealt with…

So, the poor Hernández and his friends certainly had an interest in that old man, and his house, just as a target, a way to get things of value, or money, to improve their life. After all, there were not many opportunities to find a job here, and not in that period, mainly for some like them who lived here, had no learnedness and came from this almost forgotten part of the town. So, they had to think of themselves in the first place.

After all, the unprincipled Hernández knew how such things did end: the lonely old man died, sooner or later, forgotten and with his corpse lying in the bedroom for weeks, or maybe months, before somebody understood that he hadn't be spotted by anyone for long around, not even at the food store, and his belongings were taken by someone who entered, the first to come the first to be served. And so, why wait any longer? If that old man really had some money, and objects of great value in his house, he didn't need them anymore, at present. And if he really was ill, or was dying, he wouldn't need them at all soon.

Those objects were much better, and really much more useful, in their younger hands, for buying drugs, for beer-ups or the likes. Not for an old man like Mr. Grub, what should he do with those things given his age, after all…?

Hernández had kept an eye on his house in the last three weeks, continuously. Well, not day and night, of course, but just at the right times of the day. And he had been content with finding that his way of life was really the same, morning after morning. He got out for buying food at the local store at about 10:00 AM, every two days, for his provisions, then he was back at 11:00 more or less; he ate at 1:00 PM every day, and then stayed in his sitting room for about three hours, probably falling asleep or the like, and then he got out of the front door to spend some time in the garden, having a breath of air without cleaning the ground, before the moment for dinner came while watching the surroundings—what did he have to watch, anyway? Hernández knew that there was not much to see around, the place was always the same. Not much happened to him, and he never did something unusual, nor modified his pointless life. And that was good if the three didn't want to have surprises when they had made their move, and tried to steal his personal belongings at home.

One day the boy remembered having heard their female friend of the group, called Jouna, saying that the house of Mr. Grub just gave her a bad impression, and uneasy feelings, in a way. Well, she was a follower of those sites online that had texts, and videos, about some dismal, and fabled places in Seattle that were of ill-repute. Think of University Heights Center, to make an example, that back in the day had been a school, home to a dead young boy who might still roam the hallways. Strange noises, children's laughter, and other curious sounds were said to have occurred there also when no children were present. Then, she spoke at times even of the former Harvard Exit Theatre. Today it was a Mexican consulate and other office space, but had long been a popular destination for people searching for the paranormal.

To those stupid talks Hernández had really no difficulties at replying that she had to stay calm, as entering that house unseen would be easy to the three of them, the same as take what they found and later on they could just go downtown to party and drink from pub to pub with the money they had filled their pockets with.

"You'll see, that is going to be perfect!" had said Hernández clapping both hands over his short nose and lips while looking at her in a funny way.

"Be it as you say, Ferdo…" the blonde girl, her hair long and dirty, had retorted calling the boy using that peculiar nickname he was known by among them "But that place makes me shudder…"

"Don't worry…it isn't going to be the first time, and it will not be the last one…" the boy sneered, making his right hand run through his hair while just slicking a few curls away from his face by means of the other forearm. "We'll find what we need inside and will go way richer than we are now. For some time, we'll have money to spend." Then he kept laughing in his now-all-smiling face.

So, things went on as usual for the following two weeks, with no visible changes about the behavior of the old Mr. Grub. And the three, in turn, kept looking at that house from afar. After all, they had nothing else to do, and were just waiting for the right day to make their move, undoubtedly.

Only one day something different happened: a young man of about 19 entered the house and was welcomed. That newcomer stayed inside for about three hours, then left. The three young ones didn't know much about the people that the old man might know, as usually no one came to pay him a visit. They had been wise enough to wait for enough time before acting or they might have selected the wrong day of the week when that unknown individual had come.

They didn't know why the newcomer had arrived on that day, and they were aware that the house proprietor had no sons, and no other members of the family. Might that one be a call-boy? Like a call-girl? Was it possible that the old man also was a bloody pervert that had spent some hours with a much younger individual for a payment? Everything was plausible, but the fact that the boy—who had looked very tall, well-dressed and behaved warily until he got inside—wasn't seen over the course of the following days ruled out the chance. Then, when the two weeks were almost over, that same young boy of about 19 appeared again and came in, and this made them change their plans. 'Bloody pervert, you are buying again sex with a boy, aren't you?' Hernández had thought in a disappointed look while shakily moving his hair back. This is why that same night he told his two friends that they had to make their move soon, before that unknown boy came another time to that house. Of course, Hernández had asked around, and it was certain that that newcomer hadn't been someone sent from a local store as he hadn't brought him any shopping bags nor other things on both occasions. So, the doubt still was in their young heads, anyway...

But whatever he might be to the old disgustful Mr. Grub, there was no time to waste. Before he might be there again, they had to do what they had long had in their mind.

The only thing that was important had to be that the young man didn't come another time at the wrong moment, when they had planned on entering unseen that house. And, if he really was a call-boy, that was involved into male prostitution, it was improbable that he might arrive just at the hour the old man was outside for shopping as that was exactly the time the three had chosen to go in and hurriedly steal what they'd find inside the rooms, the more the better of course.

But, when they were almost going to step inside, having set the day to do what they desired the next morning, something occurred that make them change their mind. At least, for a while. In fact, the old man didn't exit the house that day, and he didn't do that even the subsequent few days… Guyader and Jouna also told Hernández that, maybe, he had been not well attentive as the old man might have been brought to the hospital at night if he had fallen ill, or that he might have left for some time, for his reasons. But it was improbable: they all knew that Mr. Grub never moved away for a full day from his house, and if he had been taken aboard an ambulance someone who lived in the surroundings would have seen it, and known. So, it had to be something different. And, at that moment, they understood that something bad might have occurred to him: maybe the old man had eventually died. And now his corpse lay inside somewhere. If this was the case—and the lights inside that seemed to be always switched off made them think that way—they should move soon, before policemen or medics came one day to find the lifeless body of the proprietor. Because, from that moment on, it would be lost any chance to enter unseen to take his money, and his objects of value, of course!

And the three would have regretted this forever…

The present winter temperatures looked milder than usual, also with below-normal precipitation and snowfall, so far. The coldest periods in this area usually occurred in late December, from the last day of that month into early January, the same as the snowiest periods, more or less.

Truth be told, there didn't seem to be much snow around except some small low heaps here and there, something that made you almost forget that the previous week had really brought a bad weather. But now things were good…

Great for a night of stealing! But the three had to be cautious not to put their feet on that snow if they didn't want to leave revealing footmarks around anyway.

All the boys were equipped with their flashlight, and Hernández–the same as Guyader–had brought along their tools for housebreaking without making too many undesired noises. They didn't spend too long in the open under cover of the darkness as going into through one window was easy enough. The ground floor they entered wasn't in order, after all they did expect it. How could have it been differently, as the outside of that building and the garden itself were a mess?

Once inside, the wary Hernández looked at the other two then whispered in a low voice, eyeing them "No one here but us…" After some moments, he added "We can take for ourselves everything we like…"

The dark-hair Guyader and the girl sneered as if they had just been told they were entering a funny theme park, in a way…

But, as it always happened, when you most desired to have something done easily, not everything went as planned. In fact, after about half an hour they had been searching the bedroom, the sitting room and the entrance itself, the three thieves hadn't found anything really valuable so far—except a few old watches—though they had filled their blousons with everything interesting, ornaments included, they had spotted and put their hands on.

Hernández didn't seem really content with what he had put his hands on so far, the same as his fellows, undoubtedly; then, his eyes spotted something in the far corner of another room that appeared to be almost unfurnished except for two worn armchairs.

"What's there?" the boy wondered while pointing at it by means of his flashlight "That seems to be an old door to a basement…there's more to search…"

"Do not even think about going there!" Jouna, the girl, warned him. "We didn't even find where the body of Mr. Grub is in the house, if he's really dead and didn't simply leave this place…"

"I would have seen him if he had moved away during the week. I kept a watchful eye on this building! If that dotard has died, what if his corpse is behind that door? Maybe below, who knows… We came here to get money, or things of value…and as we didn't find anything really very good in the house, do you like to go out with nothing really of use in your hands? So, let's go downstairs and see if we can take anything better there…do you see what I'm saying?" Hernández replied almost being upset in a hurried tone.

"Ok, ok…maybe you're right, and maybe you're not…I don't like the air I feel in this place…I don't like this house…"

"Don't be afraid…the house shares the same revulsion we had for Mr. Grub when he saw him outside…the two were perfectly in accordance, given this run-down look of these rooms, weren't they?" Hernández sneered.

The old and worn door was locked—and that made the thought—that there had to be something important past it… - grow deeper in his mind— but it wasn't difficult to him to find a way to open it. So, the boy found ahead a sequence of steps leading to the basement and the three followed him going down the stone stairs, keeping themselves silent from that moment on.

The dim lights glowing inside two electrified glass bulbs, once switched on by the boy, had a short life of their own and soon flickered out into full darkness. But Hernández had his small flashlight with him, obviously, so didn't feel dejected and he immediately turned to it again so as to make the way before his eyes just a bit clearer, anyway. He knew they had to be on their guard from that point on, and in fact he attentively kept watching into any shadowy corner ahead though the area was discernible only insmall part, and with many difficulties, it had to be acknowledged…

The temperature seemed to really drop within a few steps down. "Is anyone there?" he called, turning his good ear to potential noises nearby.

Of course, as expected, no one replied to his words. So, the three went on. Hernández could feel the anxiety of the face of the girl at his side, but she had always been a bit afraid of everything unknown, so this didn't worry him.

In the end, when the sequence of steps—that had sounded like worrying gunshots until they left them at their back—brought them to the floor of the basement, the place smelled like earth, but different from a hundred other dark and shut-up sites underground they'd been in their lifetime. And here, within that empty space below with no chairs and no equipment around, they found something really strange. Curious looking, in reality…

"What is it exactly?" Hernández asked in a surprised inflection, glancing over to where the very unusual thing with the partly metallic–gold coloration stood against the wall. His flashlight pointed to that object got strange reflections as the light touched its shape on the upper and lower section of all of its length.

"I don't know." added the girl in a long aghast look. That tall thing, taller than the tallest boy in their small group, seemed composed of multiple hardened tooth-like layers, strange structures made of unknown material. Others appeared, instead, to be almost leathery segments, wrinkled and also very dark, in a way, strangely encased in thin flexible concentric rings that made those portions look less hard, almost softened. Its strange shape was that of a very big egg, or a wide receptacle, something like that. *A very big chrysalis with a coating made of a rough texture maybe?* Jouna didn't know how that similarity had come to her mind, in the end…She probably had watched too many pirated Horror TV series.

"What now?" Guyader asked, then he grumbled turning to the point Jouna was now staring at and saw it. "This house becomes weirder and weirder by the minute…"

"That thing, well…it looks like a prop…you know, one of those inanimate objects built by sculptors that actors interact with in a movie! Maybe it comes from some old Sci-Fi or Horror movies and might be valuable…" Hernández said.

"I am not sure…" Jouna proved to be uncertain, and doubtful. "I've never seen anything like that…"

"I, too, never watched all the movies in that genre from the 60s, I mean, they are outgone…but it might be something that appeared in one of those…What else could it be? Aren't you expecting that a big butterfly is enclosed in it and comes out soon once grown up into the adult form? Or maybe an incredibly large-bodied monster with additional legs or arms and a long, slender neck, appearing from a sheltered state or stage of being or growth, like those old movies showed off?" the boy made fun of her, then kept looking at it while making a face.

"What if it isn't a prop as you called it…? Why the house owner kept it here, how did he get it in the first place, anyway?" Guyader stared at his fellow.

"We have always imagined that damn' Mr. Grub had to be wealthy despite the bad appearances and his worn clothing of everyday…what if he worked in the movie field in the past, and kept it when he retired? Maybe he himself built that object and then he brought it here. We should just find out what kind of Sci-Fi show it comes from…" Hernández asked them.

Some moments of silence followed his words.

"What if Mr. Grub himself is in it?" the worried girl let her voice be heard clearly. "We haven't found him yet in this house so far…And we don't know what happened to him…"

"That can't be…I'll show you…it must be some plastic materials, or the likes, well made and realistic for sure…" and that said the boy moved on to get nearer that strange object situated in the same room. "Give me a moment alone."

"Don't touch that thing…What if something, whatever, is protected by that strange outer shell?" Guyader warned Hernández, but it was too late. His curious mind had already had the better of any feeling of fear, or disgust, he might have in him at that time.

And, as his hand reached that object, something started to drop from its unusual surface to the floor at once. A large amount of strange dust precipitated. Such small pieces looked like nothing more than desiccated insect remains…and the fall of other pieces continued.

In a way, it was just as if the unprecedented big chrysalis-like object, or what the hell it was, had burst open as soon as he had touched its strangely wizened surface. The boy smelled an unknown stench if his nose on his face—that appeared as if it was turned into a surprised expression—was a truthful indication.

It all really looked like one of those bad scenes you could see in a sort of Horror movie from the 1960s…But that wasn't a movie, and it all was surely real! And they all were in here…

Jouna almost choked in her spittle.

Then, two hands, followed by a figure started emerging, the size of a man, a tall man. His long fingers seemed to be using a semi-fluid liquid which in a matter of moments softened the shell of the chrysalis-like thing as if to help him make his way out in the end.

Having emerged from the chrysalis, or whatever it really happened to be, a strange adust voice was heard "You did not intend on being here, but you are here…"

The three backed off a few steps and almost called out, instinctively and out of fear, of course.

The man—because he was a real man!—-that came out started slowly shaking his bony legs and arms, his skin white and pale as the moon when it shone at night, just as if he was just testing his partly-modified, and renewed body. But there was no moon outside now, as it had gone behind the clouds, while that slim figure was before them three, and his very clear, pasty appearance almost left you over-awed.

"What the hell! What monster are you?" Hernández was the only boy of the young ones who dared speak, anyway. But he was uncertain, as if all his boldness he had when he had entered this place that night seemed to have really disappeared now, simply breathed out of his mouth and nose in a moment, by all means…

"What…are you!" the girl exclaimed, too.

"I live here…this is my house…" the man-like figure said in his strange tone letting out his words. "And why are you here?" Then, the remains of the semi-fluid liquid being on his very pale skin was dropped to the floor and the unusual gray dust on the rest of his legs and feet fell. So, his features became more vivid, and almost recognizable, in part. And a sort of shock followed.

"No, it's not possible…it can't be!" Guyader cried out.

"But…It looks like…It's not exactly like Mr. Grub…" Hernández said "But it's him, though he is different now! Younger, and taller…"

"Mr. Grub, you said? Well, that's the offensive nickname I was given by the locals, and by children like you…" the man sneered, and stared at the others in an interested look, his voice becoming more and more comprehensible. "When the moment comes about after 80 or 90 years from the last time, those of my own kind cover themselves in a hard case, call it a chrysalis, like the remains of it you now see here, and enter a stage of huge transformation. During this stage, inside the chrysalis, we rejuvenate our tissues, get better and younger legs, and other parts of our body. Only once we are completely developed, again, the chrysalis opens, and we are re-awakened, using our stronger arms to help make our way out…Then, we just need some moments to harden our new build."

"I can't believe this…no one could! "Hernández exclaimed.

"Actually, my own kind has been around for longer than you could expect. We were called *Larvae* among the Ancient Romans, in a land past the Ocean, and they thought of us as shades, or spirits, creatures that were what was left of the restless dead in the old Roman religion. But we're Undead! So, they called us that way from the term *Larva* meaning Mask. Before we appeared among the Ancient Romans, even the old Greeks had some legends about us…Strange to think that, according to those peoples, the few like us were born in the afterlife if the corpses weren't given a proper burial and were associated with the darkness. The fact is that we don't need any burial, as we come out of a new chrysalis, from time to time, living our unending life thanks to our rejuvenating ways…"

"This is unrealistic…Apeshit! Damn man, you're just making fun of us. This has to be a trick! Where's the real Mr. Grub? Or did he die, and you are his son?" the girl addressed the figure in an angered speech.

"It seems that you can't believe what you have before your eyes, boys…" the man laughed, and kept staring at them.

"No, Jouna…he's right, look at his eyes…it's the same Mr. Grub we knew, he's simplyyounger…though I don't know how it's possible anyway…" Hernández told the girl.

"Maybe you start to figure it out…"

But Hernández kept talking and insulted the other "You monster…whatever you really are, maybe you just are a vampire-like creature! And you're a pervert that goes with young boys!"

"Me? A monster? Or a pervert…? Also a vampire? Why are you telling me this? Ah, I see…you kept an eye on my house, and you spotted that young one that arrived here some days ago, and then again…you're really wrong…he is one of my own kind, he has previously undergone his modification, and he came here to bring me new documents, after the change, to be used for my new life…so, nothing perverted…only something necessary…now you know, but you are not be revealing this to anyone, of course. To my eyes it's you, the humans, who are some monsters…some short-lived creatures that can't be rejuvenated and simply end up dying, one day, forever!" the previously old —and now younger man—who was the owner of this house uttered, and a sneer was on his mouth that was showing off some teeth of worrisome length, and very unusual, anyway.

"What do you want…from us?" Guyader faced him, but he immediately backed off showily.

"The question is, in reality: what did you come here to do? I know, you feculence probably you entered only to steal, the things those like you usually do.… You know, you told me that you thought I might be a Vampire. Though I'm not exactly like that, **I and the others of my kind prey on humans anyway**, we eat those like you at the start of our new life cycle. …So, you were good to come here just when I just awakened from my chrysalis….as you see now my skin is not wrinkled anymore, and I feel much better than when I looked older. I'm also faster, much faster…" Mr. Grub simply said." I also need to eat soon. The regenerative method is really painful, and requires requires much energy. It's capable of creating a powerful field made of different energies all around my body for the amount of time needed. Later on, I will regain part of those energies lost. So, you look like the perfect food for tonight…Not just your blood, indeed, but your organs, your tissues and even your skin. Young, healthy, and tasty I imagine….I'll see soon! My kind and yours usually go different ways for most of our lives, and only once in a while our worlds collide. Today is one of those moments, very bad timing on your end…"

The three intruders stepped back, terrified. Actually, the young ones understood they had become the prey of that day, the designated victim of that monstrous creature. The girl let out a desperate cry that was heard perfectly across the whole darkened place. But no one else was there to listen. The moon was briefly glimpsed through the clouds as its brilliance became visible from the very narrow awning window of the basement on the opposite wall. The unending movements of some dark trees under the spin of the night wind in the street outside reminded the three of the strange, unsettling eyes of that man who stood there.

"Humans have that well-known saying, that 'also in the darkest circumstances there is alight'. But this is maybe the last light you're going to see…" the proprietor of the house uttered as he stared at the faint moon outside for a very short while "Parts of your bodies, the skin and meat they are made of, will be a part of me soon, and they'll be living in me for longer than any man. Though, your insides will turn to liquid. But you will be part of something bigger. And better. You should be honored, really. So, let's have it done at once…I have a lot on my mind." Then he moved on faster than the three humans might ever expect, undoubtedly. And everything went from bad to worse, anyway.

"What are you doing?" Hernández tried to oppose, keeping his flashlight with both hands as if it was a weapon, in a way "Go away!"

Guyader, the third boy, moved sideways and then cried out "No! Don't…"

But the two and the girl had obviously no means and weren't strong enough to fight against such much more powerful creature, and would never be allowed to exit that wide basement alive.

"You're not in control here…" the individual that once was called Mr. Grub told them. And his claws reached the first of the boys, tearing apart his facial features and the middle of his right arm. Soon he had a lot of blood on his hands that looked as good as new. That terrible smell of blood. The three knew that they were going to fight an unwinnable battle against something they didn't really comprehend. "I figure it's time to show everybody what I can do…Don't worry, it won't be long…"

Then, the flashlight fell to the floor and only the faint rays of the Moon outside partly revealed the movements of the figure that had once been Mr. Grub and how he was busy eating the remains of the three young ones in his basement.

The end of the boys had started as soon as the three had approached the strange otherworldly chrysalis of one of those nocturnal hunters most of Humanity had long forgotten that really existed, though they couldn't have imagined it at the beginning, of course. Nor how painful, and cruel, the way their death which had soon to come might really be, for sure…

It had to be said, they had come here at the best time to him, but at the worst to them, of course. Because, as the proverbial hawk killed because it was his nature and a man because it was his pleasure, a creature like him did it for both reasons.

MR. GRUB

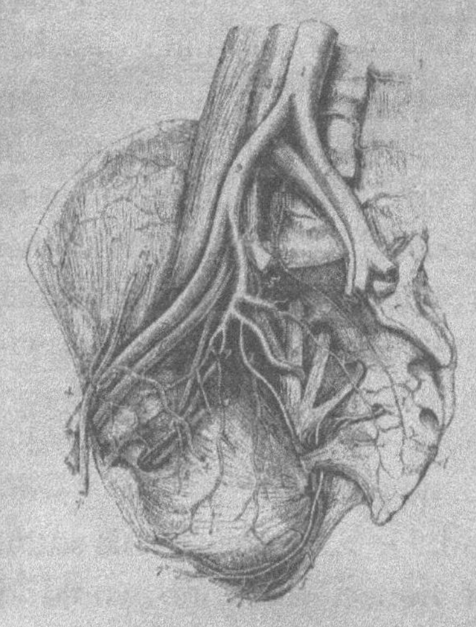

Those Who Feel No Pain
Sirius

He was 'The Mariner' even in his own mind, because Clark was a name given to a blacksmith's boy with no family. When he made submissions to medical journals, he signed his name '*M.*' which they still ridiculed, despite never once having published his writing. Amongst themselves, they spoke snidely of his work and claimed it was a depraved marriage of alchemy and necromancy. They named him an occultist and a heathen and banned him from both public and private medical halls. Nothing of what they said about him was true. His work was an empyreal science endorsed by Queen Victoria herself. She had named him, in a public document, as being a man far ahead of his time. That document was lost in archives where he was denied access, but he knew that it existed. He had seen it with his own eyes long before it disappeared.

Simone was not someone he would go so far as to call his colleague, but he was earnest, and he stuck around. He was green in his studies and had the sort of honest face one would trust to go through their finances. He would have made a lovely banker's clerk or some sort of accountant, but he did not have the brains for anatomy or the stomach for surgery.

Even so, he was poking at the body on the table, visibly marveling at the soft graying flesh that gave underneath his fingertip and did not spring back up when he pulled it away.

"So, what is this project?" Simone asked. He drew his finger down the body's sunken sternum and traced it all the way down to the navel. He placed his fingertips against his nostrils and inhaled, frowning. "What is this? Oil?"

"It is *wax*, like what you use on a ship," the Mariner set his teeth and shooed his companion away. "This one is old; I need to throw her out."

"Devilishly old," Simone muttered. "The stench of your work is pungent beyond bearing."

"And yet," the Mariner sneered, "you stay."

"Well," Simone shrugged, poking at the corpse again. "I am used to it."

"Stop that," the Mariner picked up a gleaming scalpel and waved it in a vague threat. "I will dispose of her later, but for now, I need the tail."

"The tail…" Simone turned his head to look down the length of the table. "That is rotten, too."

"Not so far gone as to not be of use," the Mariner set the tip of his blade against the tight black stitches that bonded the dead woman's waist to the silver oarfish's skin. "And you would be surprised at how much harder it is to come by a fish of this size than a usable human body."

"I would believe, at least, it is far more expensive." Simone admitted. "How much do you pay your gravediggers, and then how much do you have to pay your fisherman?"

"Bodies are cheap, it is the labor that costs," the Mariner said. He kept his focus on slicing down the stitches, cutting as precisely as possible so that the tail was not ruined. "And you would not suppose, but a graverobber thinks highly of his trade. Too highly!" He severed the last stitch. "Make yourself useful and help me carry this over there."

Simone did not argue. He stuffed his hands underneath one side of the oarfish tail and lifted at the same time as the scientist. Neither said a word as they moved it across the room and it hit the new table with a wet, dull thud.

"Strewth," Simone swore, "that smells vile. What now?"

The Mariner passed over his needle and drew his lips back to bare his teeth. "Start stitching."

Simone took the needle obediently.

"I have marked along where you need to go," the Mariner said. He clasped his hands together and pivoted on his heel, turning his back to his colleague. "After that, she will be ready to be submerged."

"You repaired your Labor Tank, then?" Simone asked from behind him.

The Mariner sucked on his teeth. "The glass only needed to be patched. It was the Hieronymus jelly that was contaminated." His own concoction of human birthing fluid, mercury, and saline water with a generous splash of formaldehyde. The resulting mixture was thick and almost lavender in color, and it emitted a soft phosphorescent glow that could be seen even underneath the tank's heavy canvas covering. "Are you nearly finished? I am not going to be able to stand much longer."

He could feel Simone's eyes on the back of his head, even as he worked to unroll the canvas back from the tank.

"You could use your chair," Simone pointed out. "You had it made for a reason."

"It limits my functionality," the Mariner said, "you cannot saw through bones from a wheelchair."

"You can," Simone said mildly, "maybe you ought to try."

"When I want your opinion, I will ask for it," the Mariner snipped. Even as he did so, he had to grasp the edge of the take. His knees were getting weaker, and his hips were already screaming in protest. Long hours worked alone made it easy to forget how much pain he was in. The presence of another person, somehow, always brought on a new degree of awareness that he hated. "When this is successful, my name will be at the top of every medical journal worth its salt in London."

"Mermaids boiled in a tank," Simone snipped a thread. "What next?"

"After that, there will be no limit as to what I can do," the Mariner finished rolling off the canvas and it crinkled as it bunched up heavily on the floor. "There will be money hemorrhaging from Her Majesty's purse. She endorses me, you know."

"I know," Simone said. "You have written her enough letters."

"She trusts my work," the jelly in the tank had an odor all its own—like a fetid wound. "I will prove that I can bring the dead back to life and create an entirely new creature all in one stroke. There will be mermaids in the Thames, mark me. And then, what do you think that will prove? Imagine what she will realize I can do for her!"

Simone sighed. "This is about Albert, still."

"It is always about Albert," the Mariner's nostrils flared as he drew in a deep breath, still clinging to the side of his tank and looking into the depths. He had to sit, but he was so close to finishing. His new creature would have to float in the tank for days. Once she was submerged, he could rest. Not before.

"God rest him," Simone said. "Between us two, I do not know if he wants to be brought back to life."

"It is not what *he* might want, or even what *we* want," the Mariner growled. "It is all about commission, and what Her Majesty will give for…Simone," his voice faltered a bit, "I need my chair."

Simone stopped what he was doing. The Mariner could hear his short, smart heels crossing the room and grabbing the wheelchair. The Mariner had been using it for under a year, and had spent almost the last of his hoarded pennies on making certain it was a comfortable seat. It had a red velvet cushion and a polished brass frame—he almost opted for wood, but wood would get ruined, and it was no good to him rotted. The frame itself had a few curls and swoops in places where they might not have been necessary, but if he ever had to appear in front of Victoria—he wanted a chair that could represent him well as a successful man of science. One day, he would have one that rivaled the throne.

Simone wheeled the chair over and reached down to pat the cushion, making sure it was plump and ready to be received. "Here you are," he said softly, "just behind you."

The Mariner ground his teeth. He hated Simone's soft, pitying tone, but he sat down regardless. It was a great relief, and his knees thanked him with a rush of relief. He still felt as though something was grabbing onto his tight calves, but he knew that tension would ease. The Mariner took another deep breath and nodded, resting his hands on the wheels and turning himself around to inspect Simone's work.

"Your stitches are very good," he said, glossing over his own discomfort for the sake of inspection. "Your work is always very neat. Very clean."

"Thank you," Simone said. "I can get her to the tank by myself."

"The tail alone weighs more than you do," the Mariner scoffed. "I will be fine. Just give me a few moments." He moved a strand of dull, straw-yellow hair away from the corpse's milky eyes. "I am hoping that a little life will fix her coloration. Else, the Thames is going to be full of stinking, bloated mermaids." He shook his head. "I wonder if God ever had to go through so much trouble to make His creatures beautiful."

"I would not know," Simone said. "I was not there."

The Mariner sucked on his teeth. "You do not know how often I have thought about climbing into that tank and letting myself float for a few days. Water is the only thing that stops my bones from aching as they do. I think that is why mermaids must never feel pain."

Simone gave him a long look. "Perhaps," he allowed.

"Water is the only thing that keeps me warm," the Mariner could not stop himself once he had started. There had been too many days alone, and Simone was the only one around to listen. "Even on the hottest day of the year, I could be freezing cold, and shaking and vomiting—and nothing can cure it, except a hot bath. Which I often have to draw myself, when I can hardly walk. Do you know what that is like? These burns on my hands are not the marks of alchemy or a scientist's experiments, they are from the copper kettle and the countless times I have dropped it when doubled over in pain."

"You should get an assistant," Simone suggested softly. "Someone who can move in to help you."

"When the Queen sees what I can do, there will be more than enough money for me to hire an assistant," the Mariner said. "Until then, no one comes here. You are the only one who does—God knows why."

"I have to wonder," Simone said. His tone was still soft, his eyes still tender. The Mariner growled.

"Do not look at me like that!" He snapped.

"I would stay with you," Simone said, "if you asked."

"Oh, yes," the Mariner scoffed. "When my bones are too weary to hold me up and when my arms shake and I shit black tar—when I need to be helped to my wheelchair and when I need my food made. Not to mention there are a dozen other tasks that do not require any sort of skill—such as handing me things from a high shelf." Disdain and shame for his own state made his stomach churn, and he knew if he kept talking, he would be in no shape to continue his work.

Simone held out a placating hand. "I did not mean any insult," he said to smooth it over. It was an offer. That is all. It stands as long as I am near— you can call upon me anytime."

"We will see," the Mariner sniffed. He looked over at his mermaid stretched out on her long steel table. Soon, she would have an entire brackish river to swim in. If the jelly did its job. If he really was the scientist he knew himself to be.

"All right," he said after a moment. "I think I am ready." He had to stand before his legs got too accustomed to sitting, or he would not be able to lift.

Simone nodded and extended a hand. The Mariner accepted it and stood. Together, they put their hands underneath the mermaid's body and hoisted her up for her short journey to the tank.

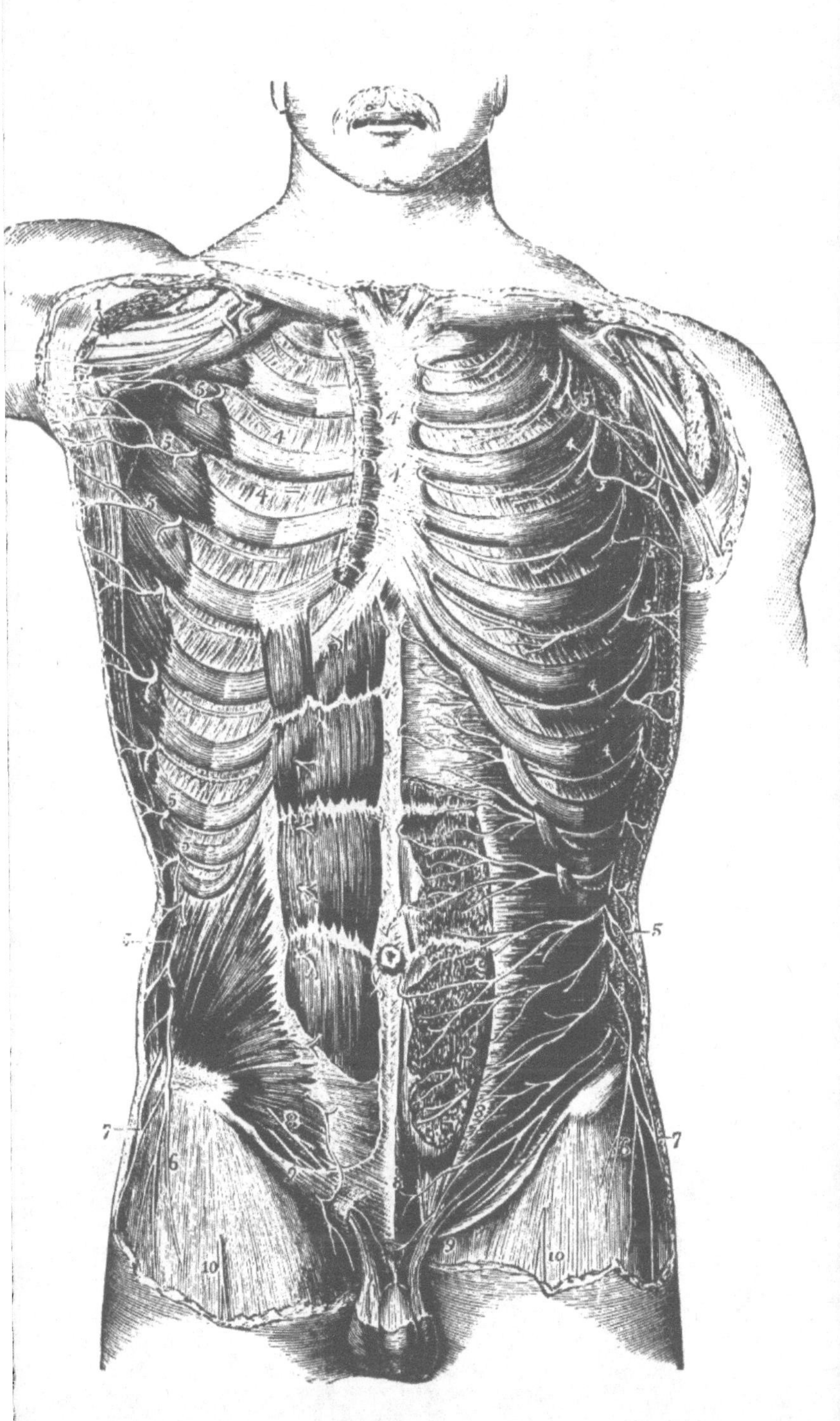